HINDSIGHT

PETER DICKINSON

PANTHEON BOOKS, NEW YORK

About the Author

Peter Dickinson was born in Zambia and educated at Eton and King's College, Cambridge. After graduation, he joined the staff of the British humor magazine *Punch* where he worked for seventeen years, leaving as assistant editor. At forty he began a career as a mystery writer. His first two books were awarded the British Crime Writers Association's Golden Dagger Award, and each succeeding book has been published to wide acclaim. Among his recent books are *The Old English Peep Show, The Last Houseparty, A Summer in the Twenties, The Lively Dead, King and Joker,* and *The Poison Oracle.* He lives with his wife in London and Hampshire.

The Library of Congress catalogued the first printing of this title as follows:

Dickinson, Peter, 1927–
   Hindsight.
   I. Title.
PR6054.I35H5   1983   823'.914   83-42816
ISBN 0-394-53182-5
ISBN 0-394-72603-0 (paperback)

Manufactured in the United States of America

First American Paperback Edition

1

This is a murder story.

There is a nasty death, there are clues, and a solution of sorts. In that way it is no different from the type of book I have written before, or from the type of book I thought I was writing when I began.

But in other ways it couldn't be more different, because it is true. True, at least, as I have been able to make it. The death of Christopher Wither did take place.

Or rather, exactly such a death took place, but the dead man had a different name.

Damn. Try again.

I began to write a straightforward detective story, using my own prep-school days as a background. In the course of doing this—partly because I was presented with fresh information, but mainly by reviving lost memories and then thinking about them—I came to believe that the actual events in which I had taken part as a child were capable of a much more sinister interpretation than I had realised at the time, or had since thought. Not that I had thought about them much, if at all, during the forty-year interval, despite it having been myself who found the body and who gave evidence at the inquest. The reasons for this blanking-out of memory will become apparent, as they slowly did to me. They are part of what this book has turned out to be about.

Having decided what the truth probably was, I could not go blandly on with my half-completed fiction. I felt I had to get the truth down on paper as best I could. But much of the evidence for that truth was embedded in what I had already written, details and incidents I had used for decoration or to support my fictional plot. These are often the 'clues' to which I referred just now. The only answer seemed to be to incorporate the relevant bits of my manuscript into a new book.

This is why the book you have in your hands could be said to consist of the first halves of two murder stories, one working forward in time and one backward, meeting and culminating in one death. So the death comes later in the book than is normal in the genre, and I think it might help readers to have this explanatory note at the start.

I have done my utmost to keep things simple. I am not trying to dazzle the literary world with a bag of tricks, only to tell a story in the way it happened. For simplicity's sake I have sometimes compromised with truth. Take the matter of names, for example. When I started writing my fiction I gave all the characters, though based on real people, fictional names. So really all the characters and places in this book should have two names apiece, one fictional and one real. To avoid this confusion I have used the fictional names throughout. This wasn't done to protect the innocent—there were precious few of them about, it turned out. For the sake of consistency, I have also altered my own name. My novel is set in the third person, and experienced by a boy called Paul Rogers, so the non-fictional part now conforms to it and describes the discoveries and self-discoveries of a middle-aged writer also called Paul Rogers, *alias* 'I'.

That is a simple confusion, simply resolved. I myself am much more bewildered by the question how much of what I 'remember' is genuine historical fact. This is vital, because on it depends the validity of many of my 'clues'. To illustrate the problem, and also by way of scene-setting, I will begin with three brief episodes—not in fact part of my half-completed fiction—that took place during the evacuation of St Aidan's Preparatory School from Sussex to Devon during the summer of the fall of France.

First comes something that has always for some reason stuck in my mind: the memory consists of the weight and ungraspability of a mattress—black-striped ticking stuffed with horsehair and buttoned with serrated leather roundels.

As I type my thumb muscles ache faintly with the remembered effort not to let it slip as I carried it across the Second XI pitch to the removal vans. The Man was there, watching the work. He singled me out and said, 'Well done, Rogue,' as I passed. The Man was both headmaster and owner of St Aidan's. His name was Thomas Smith, M A. We called him 'Sir' to his face and 'The Man' to each other. The point of his praise was that the gangs clearing the dormitories had been organised to work two to a mattress, but being in an odd-numbered gang I was carrying mine single-handed.

That, I am absolutely certain, happened. Next comes something which I know must have happened but which I hardly remember at all: my mind-album contains only one blurred snap of a master (Mr Floyd?) coming into our compartment and telling us that the train was about to pass something which he considered to be of interest. All the rest is lost. I can imagine the journey, of course, as it pretty well must have been—the appalling continuum of noise which small boys inhabit as if it were an element necessary to their survival, like air; the excitement shading to tedium as the minutes and miles thudded by; packed lunches, eked or gobbled; the scritch and prickle of railway upholstery, noticed at first against the bare undersides of knees but soon penetrating the grey flannel of shorts and Aertex of pants; at last the colour of the earth in fields changing to red as the train rocked by, and people telling each other we were coming to Devon; Exeter station, the swaying coach-trip up through winding lanes to Paddery; big gates, a short but grand avenue, a driveway winding through timbered parkland; climbing down, coach-sick and yawning, into the central courtyard of an immense brick house.

All that is lost, but clearly true. I have even lost what must have been a moment of horror, the realisation that the boys were expected to use a row of latrines specially dug for them behind the house—of Paddery's one hundred and forty-six rooms only three were water-closets. I have lost supper that night, and going to bed complainingly on mattresses laid on bare boards (did we carry them up? I don't remember). But curiously I have not lost something which at the time I doubt if I was consciously aware of, an unnoticed change in my own relationship with the world. I had moved into a sphere of greater freedom. I think this may have been true of all the boys at St Aidan's and similar schools, but I don't suppose it applies so much outside our own over-protected class; certainly our evacuation was very different from those now sometimes shown on TV, clips from wartime newsreels of labelled children being packed into trains to escape the blitz, leaving home and parents and safe streets for the first time in their lives and heading for the appalling rural unknown; we had been through our own equivalent of that small martyrdom at the start of our first term at St Aidan's. But for boys of my age and class the war was a good time to be growing up; there were many restrictions, but these bore mainly on the adults, and that somehow created space for us which had not been there in peacetime. At home, for instance, the disappearance of fathers to the war and nursemaids to war-work meant one evening meal for the family, and later bedtimes; but all sorts of less obvious openings in our caste-built boundaries became available as adults occupied themselves with the chores of war. For me, the evacuation of St Aidan's was the moment when this change took place.

With these two episodes—carrying the mattress, and the journey—I know where I am. Both are, if in slightly different senses, true. But what about the third one? It is something I had completely forgotten until I sat down to write about Paddery. It ambushed me. It sprang, it seemed, not to my mind but to my fingertips as they hung poised above the keys of this typewriter.

Waking, stiff with little aches, and opening my eyes to see a boy in pyjamas standing at a tall, curtainless window. The boy heard me stir, put a finger to his lips, beckoned. I craned till I could see the dormitory prefect (the 'dorm prae' in the usage of St Aidan's) because you could get a drill-mark for being out of bed before the first bell. He was asleep on his mattress by the door. I slithered out of bed and crept to the window.

It must have been about half-past five on that summer morning—'all in the early pearly', as my uncle's gamekeeper, Fison, used to say when describing his visits to his snares. The dormitory was on the top floor at the front of the house. Below the window was a sweep of gravel and beyond this a downward slope of rough grass, mown for hay a few days ago; the half-dried swathes lay in ridges across it. The slope was flanked by huge, still trees, and beyond it gleamed a lake. On the other side of the water rose a ridge of bracken-mottled turf, its right-hand side screened by a small wood. Mauve rhododendrons were in bloom along the far shore beneath the branches. The whole scene was banded with thin wisps of mist.

The boy beside me touched my elbow and pointed. Something moved in the mist on the slope below us, acquired a shape, was a deer, walking on delicate stilted legs, lowering its head to nudge the mown grass. Two more followed, with fawns beside them. Then, suddenly, either the mist evaporated or my eyes realised what they were seeing and there was a troop of about thirty deer moving in the dawn silence across the ground between the house and the lake.

Something stirred close behind me, an indrawing of breath. The prefect had woken and crept up to have the fun of making us jump before dishing out our drill-marks. Then he too had been trapped by the vision.

'Whiz-zoh!' he breathed.

The three of us woke the others, making gestures of silence, and we all crowded to the windows to gaze at this Eden-world to which, amazingly, the war had floated us.

Now, is *this* true? If so, how could I possibly have forgotten it for forty years? What could have caused me to bury such a treasure and go away? I think I now know the answer.

Of course, it may only have been a dream; or I may, for reasons still hidden from my conscious mind, have invented it and then persuaded myself of its truth. It had nothing directly to do with the death of Wither—there are no 'clues' in it—but I think I can say that if it is true then Wither was murdered in the manner I will describe. Also that another and in some ways more hideous crime took place.

If I made it up or dreamed it, then this book is fiction after all.

2

I began to think about using Paddery as the background for a story because of a chance meeting with the biographer Simon Dobbs. It took place at a joint committee held by two writers' organisations to agree on an approach to the Minister of Arts about the distribution of certain foreign royalty payments. Historically there had been a good deal of feuding between the two bodies, and their lot still tended to regard us as stick-in-the-muds and we them as wild boys. But the subject was too technical for much controversy and the meeting went well, despite our efforts to demonstrate our fundamental radicalism and theirs to prove their steadiness and responsibility.

I should, I now see, have realised that Dobbs was a sick man, but I am not very observant about that sort of thing. I looked at him, of course. He belonged to the quite common category of writers who affect a military appearance; short hair, neat moustache, oldish tweedy suit, erect bearing, speech quiet and slightly clipped, big horn-rimmed spectacles. Certainly he looked tired, and the veins on the back of each large pale hand stood out like tree-roots. But he had taken the trouble to go into one specially tiresome technical tangle before the meeting, and now expounded both problem and solution with admirable clarity. I thought him a bit of a stick but, despite that, impressive.

For my part I felt a silly longing to impress him, one of those fantasies which, but for his subsequent request, would soon have been stacked away with all the other junk in my mental toy-cupboard. I don't know whether other writers of my type have this absurd yearning to feel that their work is taken seriously by men like Dobbs, men who produce what I cannot help thinking of as 'real' books—three years in the writing, six hundred pages (two volumes, even, on Oscar Wilde), index, footnotes, bibliography, nothing invented, page after page of accurately researched facts, all surmises nicely qualified; and then the serialisation of the juicy bits in the major Sunday papers, long reviews by scholars, controversies with other scholars, TV programmes, a film, even, based on the Life, a whole industry. Ah, well.

After the meeting, while we were having biscuits and tea in the half-hour won from the day by our efficiency, Dobbs made his way towards me and said, 'Weren't you at St Aidan's?'

His voice was even softer than it had been in the committee, but hardly less formal.

'That's right,' I said.

'I thought I recognised you,' he said.

I blinked inwardly, though this has happened before. Judging by snapshots I was an ordinary-looking child, with no feature strong enough to suggest that my face would become what I now see in the mirror—still ordinary, but different. Apparently something has persisted that is able to call forth recognition across four decades.

'Don't tell me you're Dobbs ma.,' I said.

'I was a couple of years ahead of you,' he said, not apparently put out that I was unable to repeat the trick he had performed.

'What's happened to your minor?' I asked, with that twinge of self-consciousness one feels on using ancient school slang, in this case our normal term for a younger brother.

'David?' said Dobbs. 'Dead, I fear. Cancer of the spleen. Three or four years back.'

'Oh, I'm sorry.'

'In Bolivia. He was a mining engineer. Lived out there. I hadn't seen him for twenty years. We sent each other Christmas cards.'

Now, here is a strange thing. The perfectly inoffensive Dobbs minor—could there have been something about him that attracted that kind of relationship, or non-relationship?

He and I had been Freshers (St Aidan's for 'new boys') together, and had almost at once fallen into a dumb antipathy, soon ritualised in a convention of never speaking directly to each other; our coevals joined in to the extent of trying to set up situations in which one of us would be forced to break the long silence, but never succeeded. We kept it up for several terms until The Man noticed and simply ordered us to stop. It was by this odd closeness to Dobbs minor that I had been able to recall that a Dobbs major must have existed.

'Presumably you were among those evacuated to Paddery,' said Dobbs.

'Yes indeed. Weren't you?'

'It would by hindsight have been a convenience,' he began, but at this point one of his colleagues, a stout and dynamic woman who specialised in gritty TV scripts about the drug-culture, pushed between us and began to harangue him about some monstrosity perpetrated by the legal department of the BBC. Dobbs of course did quite a bit of work for TV, spin-off from his researches. It was natural that the woman should want somebody of his calibre on her side, and natural that he should regard the matter as of more importance than chat about our prep school. He nodded apologetically to me and bent his long frame to listen.

In my bath that night I thought briefly about Dobbs minor and his spleen. I had had an idea that that was an organ which could be removed without loss to the system. Not in Bolivia, perhaps. Now Dobbs minor had been removed, and I sensed no loss.

Two days later I received a letter from Simon Dobbs.

Dear Rogers,

I was interested to meet you last Tuesday and would have liked to talk longer. You may not be aware that I am at the moment engaged on a biography of Steen. It was intended for the centenary, but such a mass of new material has come my way that I am beginning to doubt whether I shall make it. When I went to see Mary Benison a few months before her death she was barely prepared to admit that she had even known Steen, but not long ago I received from her executors, apparently on her instructions, four large trunks of her papers, absolutely unsorted. I cannot yet tell how long it will take me to work through them or whether it will be worth the effort.

Be that as it may, even now I foresee a need to attempt to encapsulate this extraordinary woman, if only to make sure that she does not 'run away' with my book. I seem to remember my brother David telling me that the boys at St Aidan's used to call her 'Mad Molly'. This soubriquet from some of the few dispassionate observers who ever crossed her path might be a nicely ironic way of summing up her career, but before I begin selecting material with that in mind I would prefer to make sure. Would you please confirm or deny?

I cannot imagine that MB would have thought it in her interest to have direct dealings with the type of second-rater old Smith employed to teach the boys, let alone with the boys themselves, but I suppose somebody must have seen her if only to christen her as they did. Did you? If so, would you let me have a three-line pen-portrait? And if you happen to know for sure why the boys called her 'Mad Molly', that might also be useful.

Yours sincerely,
Simon Dobbs

I guessed that Dobbs had had an instinct to underline the words 'for sure', but had decided it wouldn't quite do. Of course I knew the answers to his questions, I thought. I would bash something out that evening.

It was only when I settled down to do so that I realised how elusive all my memories were. A picture of Molly as a person was clear enough in my mind, a bright and life-enhancing image, but the actual events of the year in which I knew her were strangely vague, a kind of personal Dark Ages, though I was aware of having been happy enough throughout it. I wanted to impress Dobbs with vivid and significant detail. It was there, I felt, but refused to come out.

After a couple of evenings of this the frustration began to get in the way of the novel I was supposed to be writing. When I settled to work at it next morning I found myself quite unable to concentrate. The obvious thing was to get what I did remember off my chest, put it in an envelope to Dobbs and hope to forget about it. He had asked why we called her Mad Molly, and at least I knew the answer to that. I would start there. No, I'd better explain what the girls were doing in the garden. I . . .

My finger was poised above the 'I' key when I experienced a sort of jerk, or convulsion, in my mind, an intuition so strong that it felt like a physical event. 'I' had been the problem. 'I' was the person sitting at this desk, so shaped and altered by the years that he was no longer the same entity as the boy who ran down through the chestnut grove to Molly's Sunday teas in the conservatory. The solution was to speak of the boy in the third person, to call him not 'I' but 'he'.

It worked. It came with a rush. Before the morning was over I had written nine pages—twice my usual stint—of a novel about a boy who was and was not myself. I was entirely happy—happy to have solved the Dobbs problem, happy to be embarking on new territory—I had never before written anything that could be called autobiographical—happy in the general excitement one feels when the process of creation seems to be going well. I did not ask myself for many weeks why these urgent and important memories should have stayed hidden so long, or why, even now, I seemed only able to cope with them by using the remote-handling device of fiction.

I sent Dobbs my first instalment before the first week was out.

3

Everybody always knew how the War had started. Carreras
had begun it, by accident.

It happened on the first Wednesday after the evacuation of
St Aidan's to Paddery. Back in Brighton this would have
been a half holiday, but with compulsory cricket for everybody. There was nowhere for anything like that at Paddery,
no mown turf and little level ground. So the boys were loosed
to do what they felt like all afternoon in the hayfield between
the house and the lake. Out-of-bounds was marked by
splashes of white paint on the tree trunks down either side
and the lake path at the bottom. There was a swimming
roster, two forms at a time, beginning with Freshers and
3b.

For a while the boys mooched around, exploring possibilities. The house itself—two brick wings with a stone balustrade along the top, and a grand, bowed centre containing
the State Apartments—looked down on their rovings.
Rather, it failed to look, being blind. There was permanent
black-out in the windows of the State Apartments which
produced this effect, a deadness, an indifference, curiously
chilly even on a sunlit afternoon. Mr Stock, the duty master,
sat in a deck-chair on the gravel, reading.

The War began around Fallen Tree. Being the only object
of possible interest in the hayfield it already had a name, with
notional capitals. It must have come down some years ago
and had lost most of its bark. Two stout limbs below tilted the
trunk up at an angle, and above that the bare wood of the
upper branches rose antler-like, pale and glittering. To
prevent overcrowding only boys in 5, Midway and Schol
were allowed to climb the trunk.

Down below, the mess of timber smashed and splintered

by the fall had forced the mower to leave an island of grass uncut, which by now contained patches of nettles and acted as a barrier to boys in 4 and below, who tended to cluster around, shrilling to the privileged climbers above. Gradually they threaded pathways and tunnels through the coarse grass and in among the branches. Loose bits of timber began to be dragged free. It was thus that Carreras found his gun.

It was perfect. He never needed to do anything to it beyond tying a length of cord along it for a sling. It had a straight barrel almost three feet long and had broken off with a butt-shaped wedge of its parent branch still attached. At exactly the right place below the barrel the stub of a stout twig stuck out, forming either a trigger or a hand-grip according to whether Carreras was using it as a sniper's rifle or a tommy-gun. There were even two protuberances, not very well aligned, which could be considered backsight and foresight.

At once Carreras—a large and noisy boy who had come late to St Aidan's and somehow never caught up, though he ought by his age to have been at least in 5 by now—was out in the open rat-tat-tatting at the perfect target of the boys on the tree trunk. From this accident the War took its permanent form. The boys on the tree, though of course they shot back with pointed fingers, came late to the source of weapons. By the time they'd realised that it was worth dying spectacularly as a means of getting to ground level without loss of face the juniors had all the best guns, none of them as good as Carreras's and many only suitable for shooting round corners. The seniors took over the cover of the uncut grass and, surrounded by besiegers, fired back. A few poor guns, overlooked by the juniors, were found.

The immediate effect was to establish the balance of power essential for the successful continuance of the War. One side had better equipment and superior numbers; the other had larger, stronger and faster soldiers with greater moral authority, or at least louder voices. None of this happened deliberately but the importance of it was understood by everyone. So, in a different way, was the importance of making the War work. Nobody said, or even consciously realised, that half hols without compulsory cricket were all very well but would turn out pretty boring unless *something* was happening. That in turn meant that everybody who wanted had to be allowed in; even 3b and Freshers, when they arrived slightly mud-smelling from the lake, were recruited as spies and runners.

The first of the hay forts were already taking shape when Paul arrived on the scene. With Dent ma. and Greatrex he had started the afternoon prowling along the perimeter of white-splashed trees in the hope of spotting deer, but then had become absorbed in watching and trying to divert a stream of little red ants they had found travelling up and down the trunk of a sweet-chestnut. They were still doing this when Carreras dashed past, bent low, his gun in his hand. Tyndall and Dent mi. followed him, carrying straightish sticks.

'Hey! Minor! What does?' said Dent ma.

'Bang-bang-bang-bang,' yelled his minor, pointing his stick. 'Got you all! It's War!'

'Where d'you find the guns?'

'Under Fallen Tree. Carreras got a whizzer. No use you going—they're all bagged.'

Red-cheeked, panting, he galloped after the suddenly glorious Carreras.

Paul ran out from among the trees and looked across the slope. Mounds of hay, rolled into shape in much the same way that you roll snow into a tubby cylinder to start a snowman, were being gathered here and there, some almost complete, enclosing spaces inside which several boys lay, guns across the ramparts, blazing away. He yearned to be in one of the forts, to belong there, one of the accepted heroes; but experience told him that the worthwhile groups would already have been formed, would already have a sense of exclusion around them. All the other boys in Schol were at least a year older than he was, while those of his own age naturally ganged with their own forms. If he had a decent gun it might be different.

'Down by the boat-house,' said Dent. 'Those post things.'

'Wrong side of lake path,' said Greatrex. ''Sides, they're not buckshee—somebody put them there for something.'

'Tosh,' said Dent. 'They've been there for yonks. Anyone can see.'

In fact it was Paul who slipped across the path that snaked along the lake shore. To do so gave him an odd feeling, though the boat-house and its screening trees meant there was very little chance of his being seen. He had always been a rule-conscious child, awed by authority, but there was something different about Paddery, answered by something different inside him. An unconscious conspiracy had been somehow begun between himself and this place; he was going to make it his own, explore every track, bounds or no bounds; and one day he would creep close enough to the deer to be able to touch one.

The stakes, stacked against the side of the boat-house, were not really suitable for guns, too straight, mostly too stout, and pointed at one end. He chose the three slimmest. On the way back to the hayfield they poked the points between two close-growing tree-roots and broke them off.

Most of the hay had now been gathered. The last few swathes, right up by the gravel, were being collected by a group from 4b, but the whistle for their turn to swim went at the crucial moment, allowing Paul, Dent and Greatrex to collar what was left and set up a fort. It was only when they had half built it that they discovered they were on the wrong side. Tranter and Fish took time off from a flanking raid on the depleted junior lines to explain the set-up. Greatrex began to gather an armful of hay to carry across No Man's Land, but Paul could see it was hopeless. It would be like cannibals and missionaries crossing a river. They would lose it all to raiders on one side or the other.

'Let's be neutrals,' he said.

'Not a lot of joy there,' said Dent.

'I mean we can keep swapping sides, join in where we feel like, make out we're allies with people and lead them into ambushes. The Hoofer's always talking about the balance of power. We've got it.'

'Good notion, Rogue,' said Dent. 'I'll collar my minor, soon as he's done swimming, tell him we're secret allies. Greaters, you sneak across and say the same to Barnstable or someone. Tell them we're only pretending to be neuts.'

'Neutrals wouldn't have guns,' said Greatrex.

'Wigwam,' said Dent.

It worked remarkably well. The three posts, fastened with Paul's left garter at the top, made a tripod against which the hay from the ramparts could be piled. There was just room for Paul and Greatrex to crouch inside while Dent sat cross-legged in the opening saying things like 'How' and 'Wampum' to the scampering soldiers. One or two groups of juniors, not for any good reason beyond the blind instinct to imitate their elders, began to build rival wigwams, and the War might have degenerated into cowboys and Indians if the bugle had not blown. (There was a perfectly good bell at Paddery, but it was reserved as a signal that the Germans had invaded. Only The Man and one or two praes were able to get more than a windy gasp from the bugle, so later on a handbell came into use.)

At the long, floating, half-musical note silence fell on the field of battle. Paul squirmed out of the wigwam to look. The Man was standing close by, on the gravel, with the bugle now at his waist and his white speaking-trumpet to his lips.

'Schol, Midway, Five,' he called.

He placed his clenched right fist on the top of his head. The summoned boys trooped up the slope, those who had them trailing their guns.

'Your sock's looking pretty dissipated, Rogers,' said Tranter.

('Dissipated' was that term's word, just as 'iffish' had been last.)

'That's because my garter leads a loose life,' said Paul.

He had been waiting for some weeks for the chance to make this joke, if possible in The Man's hearing. The Man looked up from the list he was studying.

'Not bad, Rogue,' he said. 'Spur of the moment?'

'Not exactly, sir—but first time out.'

'Where *is* your garter, Rogers?'

'Holding our wigwam up, sir.'

'Get it.'

'There's a spare in my locker, sir. Can't I get that?'

The Man glanced at the wigwam, the list in his hand, and back at Paul. He nodded. Paul ran off, aware that The Man, who had an obsession about socks staying up, wouldn't have let most of the boys get away with that, but that it was more for the sake of the joke (which would probably be going into School Mag) than to save the wigwam that he had done so. Aware, too, that he wasn't on the list in The Man's hand, as usual.

When he got back the War had re-started. Greatrex was alone in the wigwam.

'Where's Dent?'

'Learning rounders.'

'Learning?'

'It's a new sort. There's going to be a match on Sat. Another school got sent down here.'

'A rounders *match*!'

'It's a girls' school.'

'War does strange things to a man,' said Paul, employing another of that term's clichés to better effect than usual.

*

The girls called each other by their Christian names. They were rotten at rounders, though they said they always played it in the summer term. St Aidan's beat them easily on two afternoons' practice. They weren't much impressed by the forts, either, or interested in the War when everybody picnicked after the match in the hayfield (lemonade, scones with cream and strawberry jam, strangely like peacetime at home). But they liked the wigwam so Paul found himself host to half a dozen of them, one of whom, as soon as she had finished her tea, produced a loop of string and started to play cat's cradles. Greatrex, who had sisters at home and so used a bossy voice to the girls, said, 'That's not the way to do it. You're supposed to pass it to and fro.'

Cat's cradles had been a craze at St Aidan's the term before last. Greatrex took the string from the girl and demonstrated with Dent's help how they used to play it. Paul noticed two of the visitors glancing at each other and exchanging smiles.

'We play it in the dorms, you see,' said the girl called Perdita. 'And we're not allowed out of bed so we have to do it solo. Cora's pretty decent. Show them Starfish, Cor.'

Cora was a blonde with a thin face and a brace on her teeth. When she took the string she started by looping one end several times round her left hand, but after that her fingers moved so quickly, clutching and jerking like a spider killing a fly in its web, that Paul couldn't follow what she was up to, apart from making a hopeless tangle. If she hadn't seemed quite calm he would have felt embarrassed for her. At last she unhunched herself, jerked her hands apart with a quick fluttering movement and displayed the pattern she had constructed, intricately symmetrical, far more elaborate than anything possible by the St Aidan's system.

'Starfish,' she said.

Paul craned to look. During the craze he had found cat's cradles interesting because of the way the patterns built themselves up to greater levels of complexity at each turn, only to falter in the end on the inevitable but concealed asymmetry of the original crossing of strings. Then he had become frustrated by the limited and repetitious patterns available. It had not crossed his mind that by starting from a far greater initial asymmetry it might be possible to leap the logical barriers.

'Now it eats itself,' said the girl called Diana. 'Go on, Cor.'

Cora released one loop from a finger and gently strained the web apart. As she did so it unravelled in a mysteriously satisfactory way, the single looseness somehow following the pattern round and, as Diana had said, consuming it.

'Whiz-zoh!' said Greatrex.

'It makes up a bit for the rounders,' said Perdita.

The girl called Joan, sitting next to Paul, rather timidly produced her own string-loop.

'Can you teach me that?' said Paul.

'Cora's the only one who can do it,' she said. 'I'm not very good.'

'Anything will do.'

'I'll teach you Eskimos Running Away. That's the easiest. Or Tennis Net.'

'The Eskimo one. Why's it called that?'

'You'll see.'

He held his hands apart, fingers spread, and she looped the string on to them; but finding it difficult to visualise the movements without performing them herself she twisted round so that she could sit beside him, bare forearms laid against bare forearms and hands moving together like inexpert dancers.

*

About thirty girls had come over to Paddery, so Schol and Midway were deputed to walk back with them to their coach, which had been parked down beyond the main gates because the driver had refused to risk its weight over the cattle-grid. Instead of going directly down East Drive they took the lake path. As they passed the white-splashed boundary trees at the edge of the chestnut grove Paul managed to separate himself from Perdita, Joan and Dent and walk alone, looking almost eagerly around for landmarks and pathways, possibilities for later exploration. The process was mainly unconscious. He had no plan, not even a definite decision to break bounds, only a kind of dream-certainty that it would become possible. He might, for instance, be made a prae next

23

term. He was pretty well bound to be Head of Schol by then, anyway.

When the path came out of the grove it ran along a slope towards a line of trees. The lake shore curved away on the right. On the left a narrow track twisted up towards a sort of temple thing, which he remembered seeing from East Drive. It looked interesting. He would go there one day. Vaguer tracks, probably made by the deer or other animals, twisted off between bracken clumps. The line of trees when they reached it turned out to be the edge of the park. There was a ten-foot-high iron fence and a special sort of deer-proof iron gate. Beyond that the path slanted up to the left in the deep shade of old trees with very little undergrowth, only moss and ferns, until it came to a high brick wall with a wooden door in it. One of the two mistresses from the girls' school, who had been walking with Stocky at the head of the procession, now turned, clapped her hands and made beckoning gestures for the others to gather round.

'Now, girls,' she said, speaking as though the boys had ceased to exist, 'we are very lucky because Mr Smith has arranged for us to visit the famous Paddery gardens on our way back to the coach. You may think it funny that the gardens are such a long way from the house, but that is because it was the fashion of the times. The park through which we have been walking was landscaped in the eighteenth century by the famous *Capability Brown*, but the gardens you are about to see were laid out earlier. They are what is called *Italianate*. They are not *flower* gardens. They are a pattern of green and grey, like a carpet. You will see paths and statues and clipped box hedges and yew trees and, of course, water. They derive from the ideals of the Italian *Renaissance*, which Toppers and Sixth will be studying this term. Mr Stock tells me that unfortunately, owing to this dreadful war, the garden isn't *quite* as spick and span as it was designed to be, but . . .'

The two schools had separated, oil and water, the girls in a silent and attentive arc, the boys in a looser arc beyond, too embarrassed to be anything but silent too, minds almost closed, as if deliberately looking the other way while passing some unpleasantness at a roadside. Paul half-listened while the woman fluted on until the phrase 'this dreadful war' with its happy possibilities for use and re-use, emerged. He became oblivious, fantasising conversations into which he might spring it for the first time with maximum effect. At last Stocky opened the wooden door. Light and space, a kind of ordered glitter, seemed to stream from beyond, contrasting with the shagginess and shadowiness of the wood. Stocky held the gate for the dreadful-war woman and followed her through. The thirty-odd girls came next, and the boys last. It was thus that the stage was set, as if deliberately, by some invisible manipulator of puppets, for that weird eruption of female nature that first brought Mad Molly to Paul's notice.

The path beyond the gate was wide and gravelled, with lawn to the right, and to the left a stone balustrade with steps leading up to a flagged terrace behind which rose the main cause of the glitter, an enormous greenhouse with a dome at the centre. The lawn lay level for a couple of yards, sloped abruptly, levelled and sloped again, running on in a series of green undulations down the hill for almost a hundred yards to an area patterned with little box hedges round geometrical flower beds. Statues were dotted about, as the woman had said, and small dark trees clipped into cone-shapes. Paths ran down either side of the greenness, gravel where the levels were and balustraded steps at the slopes. Two women were coming slowly up the right-hand path.

Stocky and the dreadful-war woman led the procession along the top path, so that the girls were strung out across its length and the boys only just through the door, with Mr Floyd and the other schoolmistress waiting to close it, when the madness came. It happened all at once, or seemed to, though probably a few girls in the middle had begun it, but in an instant the whole troop of them, hand in hand to make a chain right across the lawn, were charging down the slope, long hair streaming; a wild whoop, wobbly with giggles, echoed between the garden walls.

'No! Girls! No!' shrieked the dreadful-war woman.

They swooped across the next level and on to the second slope. The yell changed note, the line wavered. Some of the girls were trying to stop, but the slope was too steep and the impetus carried them down, while the girls on either side of them, apparently blind to what was about to happen, gripped their hands and rushed them on. The green of the third level was not that of grass, but of duckweed. And, of course, water, as the woman had said. The same was true of the level two beyond. It was obvious the moment you realised what you were looking at. The paired statues on each of those levels were in fact fountains which, because of this dreadful war, had not played all summer and so had allowed the duckweed to accumulate into its perfect, lawn-imitating smoothness. All but two or three girls went straight in.

The boys stood appalled. Later they would recount the adventure, much embroidered, with laughter that almost prevented them getting the words out, but at the time it seemed to them a perfectly appalling thing to happen. Shame at such an exhibition, so unspeakably punished, held them stock still. The girls floundered in the mucky water, some still laughing, some screaming. Pretty or plain, shy or bouncy, they had become weed-bedraggled pond-monsters. The water must have been less than four feet deep and most of them seemed to be standing. The first to recover was a tallish girl, over on the right. She put her hands on the stone kerb of the pond, straightened her arms to heave her body up, got a knee on the kerb, crawled out, rose and stood dripping while she pushed her weed-streaked hair out of her eyes with a furious, proud gesture.

The two women Paul had seen on the path had been passing the pond while the charge and plunge took place, and now the taller of them came gently up to this girl as if to comfort her but at the last moment took her by the shoulders and shoved her back into the water, laughing. (In the boys' embroidered versions of the incident the woman's laugh was usually described as 'like a silver tea-bell', but it is unlikely that any of them could have heard it at the time. It seemed right to them, though in fact, as Paul found later, nothing like a proper description of Molly's bubbling tenor chuckle.) The woman did the same to three other girls before Mr Floyd and the second schoolmistress got down and stopped her. The moment they came on the scene she faced them, head thrown back, her face pale and smooth and her blue eyes looking them up and down with calm scorn; then without a word she walked back to her friend who had been waiting by the end of the pond, leaning on her walking-stick and nodding solemnly to herself.

It was thus that Paul saw within a few seconds of each other two apparently contradictory aspects of the famous Molly Benison, her readiness to demean herself and others almost limitlessly for the sake of what she decided was 'fun', and her ability to confront worldly powers with an indifference and dignity that seemed to derive from other and more mysterious sources of authority. It was thus too that the boys of St Aidan's, as well as most of the staff, came to refer to her as Mad Molly.

4

As may be imagined, it took me several drafts to compose a suitable covering letter with which to send this material off to Dobbs. It is difficult to convey (I won't even attempt it now) the sense of urgent excitement, of compulsion, which can be quite unpredictably triggered off in a writer by a sudden idea. I certainly didn't want to present myself to Dobbs as being that sort of writer, or person, but I had to face the fact that when a busy biographer has asked for three lines of fact he is unlikely to be pleased with a dozen or more pages of fiction.

In the end I simply told him that his request had stimulated me to write a novel about my time at St Aidan's; that I had always found it fatal to anticipate, either in talk or writing, scenes which I was planning to use in a book; and I added by way of bait, or sweetener to his tolerance, that this was the reason why I would prefer not to tell him about my regular Sunday teas with Molly until I'd got them down in their fictional form. I was a quick writer; as far as I knew nothing had been said in my hearing that could have any bearing on the relationship with Steen; and if it had, I was more likely to be able to recover it from the sediments of memory by letting it float to the surface as I wrote the novel than by deliberate attempts to dredge for it. Finally, to save him time I had put a double red line down the margin by the passage at the end which actually answered his question. This, I said, was an eye-witness account of an event that had really occurred.

So I made my excuses, all reasonably true, but disingenuous. I could perfectly well have sent him an extra carbon of the last couple of pages. But I wanted to know that Dobbs had read with attention and enjoyment something that I had written. That mattered absurdly. So I was disappointed to get a brief note from his secretary saying that he was away for a couple of weeks and would respond on his return, as soon as pressure of work permitted. Equally I was astonished two days later to receive a long hand-written letter from Dobbs himself. He had a very precise hand in the italic style.

Dear Rogers,

Thank you very much for your screed. I wish there had been more of it. It would exactly have suited my need for light hospital reading which I can pretend is work. I am in here for some extremely disagreeable and please God unnecessary tests, which should take about a fortnight. This does not quite put paid to my hopes of getting the Steen book out for the centenary, but takes up precious slack.

To get the so-called work out of the way first: my inclination is to quote in a slightly abbreviated form your description of MB pushing the girls back into the pond. As you say, it is true to at least two of her personae. But it all depends on what other material I find I have to fit in. There may even be something among her papers more suitable. If I decide to use your piece I will of course approach you formally for permission.

I am now going to amuse myself by reciprocating in kind. You presented me with material I may or may not want for my book, insinuating your fantastic and imaginative world into my world of plodding facts. I am in a position to fling a few facts about St Aidan's back at you. I hope they do not prove disruptive to the creative process.

If they do, you may put it down to jealousy on my part. Do you realise that it would, on average, take me at least a month merely to gather and organise the material necessary to produce an equivalent amount of words to what you have sent me? You seem to have taken six days in all, about what I would spend in the process of getting the words on to the paper. So the gathering and organising took you no time at all. It wasn't necessary. The stuff was there. Forgive me: almost all my work has been concerned with fundamentally intuitive artists, writers *mutatis mutandis* of your kind; and yet I know I can never hope to get fully 'inside their skins', or comprehend what it can be like to enjoy (or suffer) the processes by which their art is produced. Though I try not to let it show in my work I find this a matter of almost obsessional interest.

Well, facts: in 1947 I taught for two terms at St Aidan's. The school had by then, as you presumably know, moved back to the South East; not to Brighton but to a large Edwardian mansion near Tunbridge Wells. The experience was an eye-opener. To judge by your MS you regarded Smith as a fully charismatic figure. Hindsight is a treacherous guide, but I believe that even as a boy I took him with an occasional pinch of salt. Certainly as a member of his staff I found him very difficult to cope with.

For a start he was not a very intelligent man, but vain, jealous of ideas other than his own, and particularly jealous of anyone who seemed to be achieving popularity with the boys. He had a military view of his staff: he was the commanding officer; Stock, Floyd and Hutton were his NCOs; the rest of us privates. He would speak to us, often in front of each other, as if that were really the case. Our salaries were low, even by prep-school standards. He was in general extremely mean with money except where it concerned the boys; and even there he was only generous in particular ways; feeding them well, for instance, but not considering that he could attract better staff and thus get better scholarship and CE results if he paid better wages. I remember studying the Scholarship Boards. They used to hang in the Chapel at Brighton, and I expect stayed there throughout the war, but when the school moved permanently to Fenner Green he had them hung in the entrance hall. Yours, I think, was the only Eton Scholarship in fifty years. There had been two or three to Winchester. The rest were practically all soft options, Lancing and so on. Yet Smith was extremely proud of them.

You will gather I took a considerable dislike to him during

my two terms. I admit, with an effort, that he had an intuitive genius with boys, a real love for them which disaffected staff were wrong to write off as suppressed sodomy. I did so at the time, but now believe the love to have been much more parental than erotic. The trouble was that Smith saw himself not *in loco parentis* in the mundane sense but more as a surrogate God the Father. St Aidan's was his creation. The boys were all young Adams, doomed eventually to eat the apple. He saw potential serpents everywhere.

No wonder he found it so difficult to keep staff; you will recall the incessant comings and goings of people like myself. Only Stock, Floyd and Hutton stayed year after year. All three had the same odd relationship with Smith, a kind of despairing loyalty to him and the school. You will remember Stock as a grammarian and martinet. That was what he was, and that was all. Life for him was an exercise as pointless as translating sentences about Balbus and his wall, and the only task was to get through it correctly. He could remember the name of every boy who had been at St Aidan's in his time, but took no interest in their personalities or their later careers. In his spare time he would read and re-read the detective novels of Freeman Wills Croft, which he described as 'boring, but less boring than other books'. He had, I believe, been married, but I know nothing of his wife or what became of her.

Floyd was that tragi-comic creature, the repressed pederast. Of course in that era both the tragedy and the comedy were of a different hue from what they would be now. You will recall how the boys knew that he had favourites. For the staff he was always a soft touch when it came to getting him to take on such chores as duty master, because he preferred the boys' company to ours. He was both frightened and disgusted by his own drives and stayed at St Aidan's because he could cope with them there. His bond to Smith was particularly strong; he would not hear one word against him. Smith may have represented to him the barrier of authority which kept his urges in check while allowing him continuous

contact with the objects of his desire. I believe Smith understood the situation very well and exploited it by keeping a
good teacher on a low salary.

Both of these were dull dogs, really. Hutton was more
interesting, despite being a much worse teacher with little
patience with the intellectual limitations of children. He had
a good brain, wide interests, kept up with the arts, bought
and read books, etc. An amusing talker when in the mood.
Stock told me that Hutton had turned down a Fellowship at
some Oxford college, I think Queen's, because he wanted to
travel. He had money: you remember he used to drive that
Bentley? But something had happened to him in the first war,
a wound, but also some kind of accompanying horror. Smith
I know had been in the same regiment, and my impression is
that some years after the war Hutton simply turned up at
Hove out of the blue in a fairly ghastly state. The loyalty of
the trenches, now almost incomprehensible to us, operated.
Smith took him on. Hutton was always fully aware of Smith's
failings, sympathetic to the rest of us over the way we were
treated, but only rarely prepared to intervene. Once, after
some particularly despotic display on Smith's part, I muttered to Hutton, 'If I stay here I shall go mad.' He nodded,
accepting the remark as perfectly justified, but then said, 'If
I left here I should do the same.'

Is that any use to you? It may even, I suppose, be a
hindrance. How curiously different our tasks are, even when
we are both writing about the past; and, in the case of MB,
about the same person.

——After re-reading the above: I meant, when talking about
my problems in making the imaginative leap into the inner
world of the intuitive writer, to ask you whether you have any
opinions on Steen and his works. This is not a serious
enquiry. I am merely inquisitive.

More to the point, the woman you saw walking up the path
with MB. If as you say you went to Sunday teas with her, you
may know who this woman was. In Paris MB was almost
inseparable from a woman called Désirée O'Connell, a

minor poet, half French, as notorious for her ugliness as MB was for her beauty, but a much more shadowy figure, rumoured to be the illegitimate child of one of the literary Irishmen of the Nineties, but with no agreement about which. I ask because Steen refers to her in two letters with an intensity of loathing that comes strangely from him, though she was far from the only woman to persecute him with her attentions.

Yours sincerely,
Simon Dobbs

My reactions on reading and re-reading Dobbs's letter were extremely mixed—irritation at being classed as light hospital reading mixed with pleasure at then being considered, even *mutatis mutandis*, as a writer of the same type as those about whom he had written his own books; doubt amounting to distrust about what he had told me about the inner workings of the St Aidan's staff room, which as he said might prove a dangerous intrusion into my imaginative processes, mixed with reassurance that those processes had so far functioned well enough for me to have got my fictional senior staff fairly close to the facts (I had by then started to work on them in pages only partly presented here). There was too an odd sense of seeing my mirror image, accurately reversed, in what Dobbs said about imaginative writers and his own relation to them—it was, for instance, inconceivable that I should recall having seen his name over thirty years ago on a Scholarship Board, and presumably it was this type of knack, and lack of it, that had helped turn each of us into the kind of writers we were. I felt an idiot pleasure at the possibility of getting a whole paragraph of my writing into a serious work of scholarship. And then there were the odd little illuminations about my own past self, such as the reasons for Smith's resistance to my attempting the Eton Scholarship. But in the end I was surprised to find that the problem the letter chiefly posed was how to answer Dobbs's casual enquiry about what I thought of Steen.

Isidore Steen, Great Writer, the apposition so automatic as to be almost abbreviable to GW, in my case accompanied by the no-less-honorific GU, or Great Unread. My regular response to the mention of Steen's name was a collage of ennui, revulsion and jealousy. Revulsion was strongest. I was repelled for the very reasons that made him attractive to others—the gossip about the man drew them to the books, but put me off. I dislike that whole myth of the artist as shaman, the general larger-than-lifeness, compounded in Steen's case by his ferocious sexual energies and appetites for both men and women, as well as other forms of rumbustiousness. I really preferred to think of him as a phoney, and there seemed to me to be quite enough evidence without the chore of ploughing through *The Fanatics*. That whole business about the Life Force, for instance, which accounts for much that is tedious in Shaw—I gathered that Steen took it even more seriously. You couldn't believe that sort of thing and remain a tolerable artist, surely?

My resentment was strong enough to make me feel irritated whenever I read, say, a review or article that mentioned Steen and accepted that his early Saharan explorations had actually achieved anything, or that Baston's demolition job on the veracity of Steen's account of his own Lawrence-like exploits in East Africa during the first war had not really demonstrated that *To Live like the Jackal* was a pack of lies. I had of course read that book at Eton but unlike most of my friends had not been bowled over by it. The feeling that Steen was not my kind of man or writer was already strong.

As I say, the distaste was reinforced by what I learnt about Steen as a person. I tended to shut my mind to anecdotes of his friendliness and casual generosity to young writers short of luck or money; I assumed it was a method of getting them into bed with him. Occasionally I came across a quotation from one of his books, and I remember turning on Radio 3 halfway through what was clearly an archive recording of a talk and then listening with real interest and stimulus before learning at the end that the voice had been that of Steen. It was impossible at times like this not to acknowledge that the style was muscular and uncluttered, the point of view sane, some of the individual ideas perceptive, subtle and occasionally prophetic, and the whole approach far less egotistical than I would have expected.

Despite this I continued to resist, though increasingly swimming against the accepted current of thought. For even without the coming centenary Steen's reputation would have been enjoying an upsurge. Most parties and factions, especially those with an ecological bent, were tending to claim him as a father-figure. I had read only a couple of weeks before a piece in one of the Sunday Arts gossip columns about a film of Steen's life in the offing. (I'd had a double reason to pay attention to this—it was based on Dobbs's book, apparently, and the part of Molly Benison was to be taken by Lee Remick; I even, I'm afraid, wondered whether Dobbs's spurt of interest in Molly was motivated as much by his need to provide material for the film as by the requirements of his book. I wouldn't have minded had this been the case. Dobbs had developed great skill in financing his serious work from mass-media spin-offs, without which the books perhaps would not have existed. But I would have liked him to tell me.)

But did anyone *read* Steen? I had to go into Winchester the morning I got Dobbs's letter and parked my car behind the public library, so it was easy to check. Most of his books were in stock, and had been borrowed at least a couple of times in the previous year. Even *The Fanatics*, that great white whale of a novel, had a recent date-stamp in it. Mine had more, but then Steen had died in 1927, the year I was born. How many date-stamps did I expect *my* books to carry in 2027? Ridiculous question.

In the end I overcame the urge to pretend to Dobbs that I knew and liked Steen better than I in fact did, and simply said that I had not read enough to be able to form any opinion other than that he wrote good English.

As for the effect of Dobbs's letter on my own book, I

decided I could afford to make the Captain a bit more openly contemptuous of his colleagues and poor Mr Wither more bewildered. I had already written the scene of their first appearance but the tone could if necessary be adjusted in the re-write. As for Daisy O'Connell (I'd never heard her called Désirée, as far as I could remember), I was within a day or two of describing her first real entrance, but still had little idea whether her role would be more than that of a walk-on grotesque. That's the sort of thing I tend to find out as I go along. If I actually remembered more about her than I needed for the book I could always amplify for Dobbs on a separate sheet, as they say on the accident report forms—but not until after the accident had occurred.

I sent my next instalment off, addressed to the hospital, before the end of the week.

5

On the first evening of the Christmas term Chapel was always extended to allow all the notices to be read. They still called it Chapel, though at Paddery it took place in Big Space, as what had once been the ball-room was now called. This was the only one of the State Apartments into which the boys were normally allowed, and then only for Chapel, indoor activities on wet days, and a few other things like that. With its frothy white-and-gold décor and its painted ceiling it never felt quite gloomy enough for a chapel. You could get a drill-mark for deliberate staring at the ceiling because most of the ladies had at least one breast bare. In fact, after the first week of mild shock the boys by silent vote had agreed to ignore it, so that Venus and her attendants hovered un-noticed and unconsidered above their activities, just sublim-inally there, like all those other aspects of the adult world for which they felt they were not yet ripe.

The Man read the notices after the first hymn. First, the names and new schools of leavers, with any awards they had won—more leavers than usual as eight boys had been sent by their parents to America. Next, this term's praes; Scammell was Head Prae, though he was only in 5; that wasn't unusual, because it was important that the Head Prae should be pretty good at games; Paul was not on the list of new praes. Next, heads of forms; Paul was Head of Schol. Next, the Freshers; again, more than usual—some, like Carreras, coming from other schools, probably because they hadn't managed to evacuate to as good a place as Paddery. Then a lot of new School Regs, because of the war—things like no second helps at boys' dinner, and the tuck-shop closing. The one on which The Man laid most emphasis was the black-out.

'The Hun is just across the water now,' he said. 'Soon the

evenings will be getting dark. I have fought against the Hun, gentlemen, and I know how his mind works. He's efficient, but he's a bully, and like all bullies he's a coward at heart. You'll have read in the papers how he's been trying to bluster us into giving in by a show of frightfulness, sending his bombers day after day, but thanks to the gallant chaps in the RAF—including, I'm proud to say, not a few Old Aidanians —all he's got is a bloody nose. So now he's started night bombing, sneaking across in the dark. We've had the luck to move away from the worst of it, but that's not to say he won't be over here too, looking for targets like Plymouth and Exeter and Falmouth. He's not going to be choosy. He's only got to spot one spark of light below and he'll drop a bomb on it. Let me tell you this, gentlemen. Suppose one of you could fly up there and sit beside this Hun in his cockpit and tell him the light he saw was only a school, full of children—do you think he'd give a hoot? No, he'd be glad of the information, glad of the chance to wipe out eighty young men who in a few years' time would be doing their bit about keeping the Hun in his place. So it's up to you. Mr Stock will be official Air Raid Warden. Dorm praes will be in charge of black-out in their dorms, and form heads in their forms. The duty master will be going round outside after dark, and if he spots one chink of light every boy in that dorm or form will be punished. Understood? You are all soldiers in the war against the Hun, and this is an important part of your soldierly duties.'

Next The Man introduced the new staff in ascending order of seniority. There was an Assistant Matron, who looked friendly, and a pale young woman called Miss Penoyre who was going to teach Freshers. Two new masters, Mr Wither, who would take Senior Maths and Captain Smith who would take Greek as well as some Latin and History. To avoid confusion with himself The Man said that Captain Smith should always be referred to by his rank.

The school stared at the two men. (Matrons hardly counted and Freshers, except for the two or three older ones who would be put into higher forms almost at once, kept rather separate.) All masters were extraordinary at first sight, almost freaks. The relationship gave them such power over the boys that they seemed to stalk or creep on stage like monsters; and so some of them remained, a sense of dread and misery, or more rarely of glory and release, hanging round them always; others lost their apparent potency but never became human, reaching instead an accepted indifference, idols as it were of deities in whose power few citizens any longer believed.

Mr Wither was visibly a bit of a freak because one of his shoes had an enormously built-up sole, almost six inches high. He was quite young, pink-faced, grinning with obvious unease as he stood to be introduced. His wispy blond hair flopped sideways and his blue eyes blinked behind gold-rimmed specs.

Captain Smith was older, short and tubby. His head seemed not to belong to that body, looking too large with its high, bald brow, and too lean with its sculptured cheek-bones. Furthermore he wore a quite extraordinary moustache which bristled out sideways, as if it had been a bundle of horsehair stuck on for amateur theatricals. He too rose from where he had been sitting with the rest of the staff in a line along the wall to the left of the dais.

'It will be a pleasure to get to know you better, gentlemen,' he said, lowering his head in a curiously oriental fashion as he finished. He had a very deep voice, like a priest's or an actor's.

Paul felt a tremor run through the school, perhaps surprise that he had spoken at all or at his complete self-confidence. Later Paul wondered whether they had not sensed, with that mild telepathy common among groups of children, a tinge of mockery in his use of the word 'gentlemen'. For The Man the purpose of St Aidan's, and therefore of his own existence, was to train gentlemen who would grow into the natural leaders England required—he said so in his Leavers' Sermon at the end of each term. There was never any irony in his calling the boys gentlemen. But they were to learn that the Captain seldom spoke of anything without layer under layer of what might or might not be ironical intent, unfathomable. Certainly Paul's first impression was correct. There was something much more freakish about Captain Smith than about Mr Wither, despite the latter's deformity.

Chapel resumed its normal course for a while. Scammell read a bit of St Luke. Dormer read three collects. The boys rose for the last hymn. But at this point The Man came back to the dais.

'Since we last gathered here,' he said, 'I have learnt that the following Old Aidanians have made the supreme sacrifice. Pilgrim, J. P. C.; Wynn-Williams, H. J.; Darlington, S. V. Greater love hath no man than this, to lay down his life for his friends. We will sing *O Valiant Hearts*, St Aidan Book, number nine.'

This was a favourite hymn with everyone. They belted it out. Matron played the piano.

Schol and Midway were stacking the chairs back against the wall of Big Space when Dent said, 'Bit of a swizz, Rogue, not making you a prae.'

'Suits me,' said Paul.

'Head of Schol's always . . .'

'Honestly! I don't want it!'

'Rogers!'

That was Scammell calling from near the door, and then waiting, clearly expecting Paul to go to him rather than be shouted at from that distance. Paul lounged over, determined to demonstrate his free will in the matter.

'In the Study. Now,' said Scammell.

'What does?'

'You'll find out.'

To get to The Man's study you went through the green baize door half-way down Long Passage and came out under the stairs at the back of the entrance hall. The stairs were marble, curling up on either side of a black bronze statue of Hercules strangling the Nemean lion. Beyond it you could see the slim white pillars that supported the cupola, and then the front door, almost as large as the door of a barn, always locked now. The hall was dim-lit by one yellowish bulb, any daylight excluded by permanent black-out screens. Your heels clacked on the marble floor as you walked round the left-hand flight of stairs to tap on a shiny red mahogany door. The Man called to you to come in.

He had made the Study as like his one at Brighton as he could—the same photos of XIs and XVs were ranked on the walls, the same portrait of his father, a red-faced man in a dog-collar who had been the school's founder, hung over the fireplace, there were the same deep floppy armchairs and sofa covered with rose-patterned chintz, the same smell of sweetish pipe-tobacco and bat-oil and some large tame animal—it must have been The Man himself, as he kept no pets.

Paul found him working. The only light in the room spread across the desk-top from the green-shaded lamp. His face was little more than a presence in the shadows beyond, but his hands, their backs covered with curling gingery hairs, moved in the plane of light like animals browsing on the paper repast.

'Sit down, Rogue. You notice I haven't made you a prae?'

'Yes, sir.'

'What do you think about that?'

'I don't mind, sir. I wouldn't have been very good at it.'

'Oh?'

'I don't like taking sides, sir.'

'You can overdo that attitude, Rogue. "Once to every man and nation Comes the moment . . ." You don't think so?'

'Do you think it's true, sir?'

'Explain.'

Paul hesitated. His habit of noticing the meaning of the words he was singing had sometimes given him the giggles in Chapel, once setting his whole pew off and earning them all Sunday drills. He had thought about this hymn fairly often, because it was a favourite of The Man's—but that made answering a bit tricky.

'I mean, well, it doesn't . . . Just once, and that's all?'

'You're a clever infant, Rogue, but you mustn't be too clever. A hymn is not a legal document. It means "at least once". Everybody gets at least one go, one choice. Some of us have to go on choosing all our lives. You have a fair brain and the makings of becoming a sound chap, some use to your country when you grow up. You'll be given a lot of chances. You'll chuck them all away if you try to spend your life sitting on the fence like a neutral.'

'Yes, sir.'

Paul felt crushed, though The Man had spoken gently. The idea of being a neutral, crystallised by his enjoyment of the role during the hay-fort War last term, had given him an oddly comforting picture of himself, a way of explaining the slight apartness caused by his too-rapid climb to Schol.

'Because thou art lukewarm, and neither cold nor hot, I will spew thee out of my mouth,' said The Man with sudden emphasis.

It was obviously a quotation and—as usual when he quoted anything—it was a sort of half-question. The way to please him was to try to answer.

'St Paul, sir?'

'Not far off. Revelation. God says it to the church at Laodicea, because they were trying to be neutrals. He will say it about America if they don't join us fighting the Hun. You mustn't let Him say it to you, Rogue.'

'I won't, sir.'

'Good lad. Now, about my not making you a prae. It's not because you aren't up to it, Rogue. If that had been the case I wouldn't have told you. I'd have let you work it out for yourself. But it's because your stepfather has insisted on your sitting the Eton Schol next summer. You see, Rogue, there's a lot of competition for these plum scholarships, and that means there are schools which specialise in getting boys through them. I call them cramming schools, and I believe it's a thoroughly bad idea. Boys who've been crammed are like plants which have been forced in a greenhouse—not much use for anything afterwards. You'll notice that if you get to Eton. So I've refused to have you crammed, but I've agreed to see you get a bit of extra tuition.

'Your best chance is clearly your maths, but Mr Floyd thinks you aren't quite up to getting through on that alone, so we're going to have to pull your Latin and Greek up too. I've sent for a set of old Eton Schol papers, and Mr Wither will be taking you through the maths ones. Mr Stock says your work last term was sometimes good but often very careless, and he doesn't think it's getting any better. I don't think this is because you've been idle, exactly. Your trouble is that when you aren't interested you close your mind up. Right?'

'Well, sir, it's . . .'

'You'll have an unhappy life if you always take that line, Rogue. But for the moment we'll see if a change of approach might help. Captain Smith tells me his methods are a bit different from Mr Stock's so I'll ask him to give you a hand with your Classics. I'll let you know about times in a day or two. The reason I wanted to talk to you at once is so that you can tell anyone who asks that the reason you aren't a prae is that I don't want you distracted from the Eton Schol. To make it absolutely clear that this is the case I'm going to give you praes' privs.'

'Oh, thank you, sir!'

'Not for your sake, Rogue, but for the school's. You could easily set yourself up as somebody who was outside the bounds of school discipline. I'm not going to allow that. If a prae gives you a drill-mark I shall back him up, right or wrong. Or if Scammell, for instance, tells you to do something I want to be sure you'll be doing it as willingly as if you were still in 3a or Shell. Any nonsense about this and I shall take your privs away. Got it?'

'Yes, sir.'

'Good lad. Off you go now. Ask Scammell about the privs.'

Paul had to stand for several minutes in the shadows between the statue and the baize door, trying to master all the symptoms of sobbing except actual tears. The Man had been friendly and helpful. It would be marvellous to have praes' privs, as well as an explanation for people like Dent about not being an actual prae. But . . . could Scammell . . . no, there hadn't been time. The Man had *known*. He seemed to be able to get inside your mind and look round, like Matron looking in your locker to see it was tidy. He had known about feeling sometimes so afraid of Stocky that your mind closed up. He had known about the idea of being a neutral, much more than you had let on. He had known what Dent was saying, and how you had behaved when Scammell had called you, and about the already-forming notion that if you were Head of Schol and not a prae there wasn't much Scammell or the others could do if you chose to do as you liked. There was something appalling about having your hidden inward self understood like this. It was like being found out for some kind of rule-breaking when nobody had told you what the rules actually were. Paul spent the rest of the evening alone among the ink-smelling desks in Schol, reading *Fire Over England*, which he had read twice before.

*

Being tutored in maths by Clumper Wither was like playing a game with a friend. The Clumper adored algebra and geometry and trig, and tricks with numbers. He would chuckle aloud as he watched some tangle of letters and figures unravel itself (a bit like Cora's 'Starfish'), cancel out and come down to $\therefore x = \sqrt[3]{-3}$. His weakness as a teacher was his inability to understand how anybody could find this jugglery difficult, or boring. Within a week the boys could imitate perfectly his baffled, pathetic cry of 'But don't you see . . .' He couldn't keep order either, and he might have been ragged much more than he was if he hadn't been such a good egg, so easy to like, so nearly a boy in some ways. And of course he had the terrific advantage of his car, a little black open MG, with a tiller-knob and throttle-control on the steering-wheel so that he didn't need to use his bad foot to drive. He got extra petrol, too, for being a cripple, and he

44

drove like a racer if he took you out, making the gravel squirt from the drive as he accelerated and doing four-wheel drifts round the bends.

Nobody imitated the Captain, though there was plenty of material there, in his deep almost chanting voice and flowery speech, his mincing walk, his stillness, his sudden dramatic gestures. He was too obviously dangerous to take risks with. He had no trouble keeping order but there was never a whisper of inattention in his classes, even on days when he came in, glared at the boys and said, 'Read your books.' That was what they did, sometimes for three-quarters of an hour, while he stared out of the window at the park, though he made no bones about his loathing of the countryside. On other days he would decide to talk, walking round the room, speaking as it were to the air. He might spend a lesson telling them about Belisarius defending Rome against the Goths by a series of cavalry sorties and then give every boy eight marks out of ten for work supposedly done on conditional sentences. When he got round to the drudgery of grammar he would enliven it by giving the boys absurdities to translate into Latin—'They tell me your sister has two heads' is a simple example. No one ever saw him smile or frown.

Paul's tutorial sessions with him, like those with Clumper Wither, took place in a small, dusty room down the left-hand corridor beyond Big Space. There were plenty of such half-used chambers at Paddery; even without the State Apartments the needs of eighty boys and twenty-odd staff did not fill it. Paul brought his Kennedy and his exercise book to his first Latin tutorial. He waited, and was just beginning to fret about having got the place or the time wrong when the Captain glided in, said 'Good afternoon,' picked up the exercise book and glanced through it.

'Vile writing,' he said.

He turned a page, read a little, looked at two more, then stared for a while at Paul with his unsettling eyes, deep brown, outlined by thick and bloodshot rims. He spoke suddenly.

45

'What kind of people do you imagine it must have been who felt so powerful a need to place the verb at the end of the sentence?'

'I don't know, sir.'

'Imagine yourself in the House of Commons. You are listening to that eloquent ass, Sir Mark Cicero. He is just getting into his stride about the unspeakable behaviour of Mr Catiline. This villain, he tells you, nineteen virtuous matrons, more about their virtue all in the accusative so you know he's done something to them but what, for heaven's sake? Robbed them? Raped them? Taken them sailing? But, aha, here's an adverb, whatever he's done he's done vilely, it looks as though we're getting somewhere, but oh, no, here's a *quia* and we're plunging into the villain's motives when we still don't know whether the matrons are dead or alive . . . You follow me? What kind of a mentality can the Romans have had to regard such a sentence-structure as a vehicle of rational discourse? Do you mean to say that this is an enigma on which you have never meditated?'

'I'm sorry, sir. Mr Stock just said . . .'

'Poh! I speak nine languages with fluency. I am wanted by the police of five of the countries in question, but let that pass. I have the credentials to insist that you will never speak or write a language to your own satisfaction until you have learnt to think that language, to breathe it and to sweat it, until you regard the only rational form of discourse as including the verb coming thumping in at the end of the sentence like the big bass drum behind the band. I notice that you have a penchant for the solecism known as active-for-passive.'

''Fraid so, sir.'

'That is because you do not feel the activity of the active mood, the passivity of the passive, let alone the pregnant indeterminacy inherent in deponent verbs. You will now sit and think for five minutes about the verb *sequi*. At the end of that time you will tell me what kind of a mind the Roman must have had to believe that to follow was in some sense to have something done to him, rather than to be doing something.'

Without waiting for response the Captain turned and stared out of the window at the vista of trees winding down West Drive. You could almost tell by the way he stood that he disliked what he saw.

*

When Scammell explained praes' privs to Paul he spent most of the time talking about things like remembering to take your hands out of your pockets if there was a master around. (Letting praes walk around with their hands in their pockets was The Man's way of making sure no one else did.) Most of the privs were like that—useless, apart from conferring prestige. They weren't what Paul was interested in. But it didn't seem to occur to Scammell that a boy might actually want to go into class-rooms other than his own, or spend his spare time not playing some kind of semi-organised game. Even on walk-days he went off with the main school instead of taking the chance to explore on his own or with some other prae. So he just lumped all the privs Paul was interested in at the end, saying, 'You can go into other classes if you want to, and you don't have to stay inside Painted Trees. Don't bother the deer. Anyway they're supposed to be dangerous this term.'

It's hard to say, supposing Scammell had laid more emphasis on these last two sentences, whether Paul would have given up his idea of learning to know the park and its creatures so well that he would one day actually touch a deer. As it was, the only attention he paid was to decide that any deer-stalking would have to be done well out of sight of the school. This would mean exploring the remoter reaches of the park, which he wanted to do anyway.

During the hols The Man had got a patch of grass mown up behind the stables, large enough for one football pitch. Almost everybody got one game a week, and on the other half hol they went on School Walk. So with luck Paul would get a whole afternoon once a week, another on Sundays, and about an hour on the days when he had to play football. There'd be breaks on the other days, but not long enough to get far from the school. His first chance came the Wednesday after the start of term.

The park turned out to be even larger than he'd thought—Uncle Charles's park, which was really only a big field with trees in it, would have gone into Paddery a hundred times over. West Drive was two miles long and East Drive half a mile. There were two whole woods and lots of copses. A stream too wide to jump fed the lake, but ran out underground towards the gardens. There were some odd buildings too—the Temple on the ridge between East Drive and the path to the gardens, a sort of dwarf pagoda, painted blue, in the middle of one of the woods, and a ruined chapel on a hillock near West Gate. In spite of these features it was surprisingly easy to get lost among the hummocky, bracken-mottled, oak-dotted hollows and rises, which gave the whole park a dream-like feeling—parts of it were so similar to other parts that you felt you had somehow slid back without noticing and were going through the same experience all over again.

Around the perimeter, but outside the belt of trees which rimmed the southern and eastern edges, ran a ten-foot brick wall, which you seldom noticed because it was built in a kind of ditch, with the earth piled into a bank that ran parallel to the wall inside the park. You could say the ditch hid the bottom half of the wall and the bank the top half. The idea of course was to keep the deer in, and when Paul found it he saw that it might make his efforts to approach them enormously easier, either by allowing him somehow to corner a group, or else by enabling him to approach along the ditch and then sneak up on them over the bank.

That first afternoon he was totally unsuccessful. There were plenty of deer about, in small groups, not just the hinds which he had mostly seen last term, but a number of stags with them, splendid shaggy animals with great branching antlers; they strutted to and fro and bellowed from time to time at stags in other groups. Paul remembered what Scammell said about their being dangerous this term, and decided it must be some kind of mating season. He had a vague idea it was called 'the rut'. He had brought his gun from the hay-fort War with him to use as a staff, and he thought that if a stag saw him and charged he might be able to beat it off by using the gun as a quarter-staff. Or if he was near the wall he could climb to safety by wedging the gun against one of the buttresses and using it and the buttress-top as a step and handhold to allow him to reach the coping and pull himself up. He experimented with this, to make sure he could do it quickly, and was surprised to find that the ground outside the wall was only six feet below him.

His precautions turned out unnecessary. If the stags were dangerous, they were also incredibly shy. Before he got within a hundred yards of any group a head would come up, and then another. The big ears would twitch to and fro for a moment and then fix. Next thing the whole group would be moving away at a sort of half-run which looked quite easy for them but was much faster than Paul could have gone flat out.

In a way Paul was happy to find them difficult quarry. Their wildness mattered, not just because it was a part of the game, but because he felt it was something he needed for them, almost as though when he at last reached out to lay his palm against the quivering haunch something would flow between him and it, some blood-brotherhood be established, allowing him to take part in the secrets of that wildness and freedom. He did not think of the wall and ditch as a prison, keeping the deer in; it was more like a fortification, keeping out the tame straight rows of turnip-tops that patterned the red fields outside. The deer had the run of the wild beautiful region between the tame farmland and the tame happenings inside the walls of the school.

The nearest he came to any of them that first afternoon was by accident. He had made a wide circuit down to East Drive and was walking up towards the school when he passed the path that led to the Temple. He decided there was just time for a closer look at it before tea. The path looked almost new—it must have been re-gravelled just before the war with reddish chippings which crunched beneath his leather soles. The noise offended him after his efforts at stealth, so he deliberately picked his way up on the grass verge until he came to a small paved platform from which stone steps rose to the building. This stood on a small mound and was no more than a dome supported by eight pillars with a statue on a pedestal at the centre. As Paul was climbing the steps a stag roared close by. Thrilled by the nearness of the sound, he stole up the steps and under the dome, using the statue itself for cover. He peered carefully round the billowing marble drapery.

He saw at once that the mound on which the Temple stood must have been artificial, made by scooping earth out from the southern slope of the ridge and piling it up here. It had been done that way on purpose so that immediately below the Temple there was now a small grassy arena in which some deer were grazing, about five hinds, some half-grown fawns, and a big stag which at the moment had its back to Paul and was bellowing its challenge down over the far rim of the arena. It was gloriously posed, with the lake beyond it. The slope below the temple was as steep as the roof of a house, impossible to sneak down unnoticed, but there was plenty of bracken on either side and it might have been possible to worm nearer by going back down the steps and making a flanking attack. No time for that before tea, though, so Paul simply stood and watched.

He wasn't aware of having made any sound or movement to attract the animal's attention, but suddenly a head came up, and then another. The stag wheeled and stared. An instant later the whole troop was off over the rim, out of sight, crashing away through the bracken.

Paul looked at the statue before he left. It was a woman, Diana, probably, because she had a bow and arrows slung at her back. In her left hand she was holding up a crescent moon. You couldn't see whether she was beautiful because her face was so streaked with bird-droppings.

*

Next Sunday Paul got involved in a game of Monopoly which went on so long that there was no time for exploration, and the Wednesday after he was in a football practice which didn't end till the afternoon was half over. Still, there was time to have a go at the Temple deer again, so he took his gun, walked down East Drive and up beside the gravel path, as before. This time, however, instead of climbing the steps he turned off to the right. The bracken grew thickly here, but there were paths through it, made by the deer, probably. He picked his way along, crouching low and taking slow, small steps, crawled over the ridge, and then crept back along the other side towards the arena. Everything was quiet. The stag didn't roar once. Paul was very patient. It must have taken him half an hour to do the circuit because whenever he made the slightest rustle he stood quite still and counted to a hundred before moving on again, but when at last, now worming his way forward on his stomach, he lifted his head to look down into the arena, it was empty.

Disappointed but not unhappy, because he felt it had been a good practice stalk, he walked down the other path—a track, really, narrow and rough, without any gravel—towards the lake and then back along the lake path. He was just reaching the chestnut grove when he saw half a dozen deer coming along by the shore at a fastish trot. Quickly he slipped down through the trees and stopped behind one at the edge. Already he could hear the rapid soft tapping of hooves. He held his breath. The stag came past, only ten feet away, not looking particularly concerned. Presumably because Paul was standing still it did not seem to notice him, but trotted on without check. Five hinds followed in a close group, and the last of these seemed suddenly to recognise that the vertical object at the edge of the copse was not a tree-stump. Paul was convinced that he saw the glistening

51

round eye change shape. He definitely felt the flash of terror, the spasm of released juices that triggered the muscles to send the animal springing forward in a huge leap. Next instant the deer had fled out of sight.

As Paul was coming back up between the trees he saw that there were figures walking along the path from the boat-house, two women, Mad Molly and her friend. He realised that they must have been what disturbed the deer in the first place, and by concentrating their attention on the danger behind caused them not to notice Paul's almost-ambush. There wasn't anyone else around. He didn't want to meet Mad Molly, not because he was really afraid of her, but because she was obviously a dotty old woman, likely to do or say something embarrassing. So he waited behind a large tree close by the path, preparing to edge round it as the women shuffled past.

He was standing there, listening for the faint pad of footsteps but partly distracted by studying the pattern of deep, slanting grooves in the chestnut-bark, when a voice close behind his neck said, 'Boo!'

He leapt. There may not have been much outward move-ment, but his heart seemed to bound as the deer had, and he felt the same surge of panic-triggered energies. He managed to turn, cheeks hot, palms sweating. Mad Molly was smiling at him round the tree trunk. She had clear pale blue eyes which sparkled with the fun of it.

'How did you know I was there?' he said.

'Witchcraft, of course.'

'I'm allowed beyond Painted Trees. I've got praes', er, privileges.'

'I'm sorry to hear that. I'd much rather you'd been breaking a rule—so much more interesting. What's your name?'

'Rogers, ma'am.'

'Nonsense. You're no more Rogers than I am ma'am. My name is Mary, but most of my friends call me Molly. Your name is . . . ?'

'Paul.'

'That's more like it. Come and meet my friend Daisy. She's a bit sad today.'

Trapped, Paul followed her out on to the path. The other woman was absorbedly moving a chestnut husk to and fro with her stick, but she looked up and stared at Paul.

There was something awful about her. It wasn't just that she was rather ugly, with a flat, pale crinkled face with hairs sticking out of it, and a podgy body dressed in a lot of different-coloured fringed shawls. Paul became used to her after that first meeting and ceased to notice the effect, but there in the chestnut grove he was immediately certain that he didn't want to get any nearer.

'His name's Paul,' said Mad Molly.

'How old?' said the Daisy-woman.

'Twelve, ma'am,' said Paul.

'Twelve, ma'am,' said Mad Molly. It might have been Paul's own voice.

'I'll do that every time you use that stupid word,' she went on. 'I'll come to church on Sunday, see if I don't, and do it in front of your friends.'

'Six years still,' said the Daisy-woman.

'Before you can fight in this stupid war, she means,' said Mad Molly. 'Daisy's obsessed by the war. Don't worry, darling. I expect Paul's father is fighting away like a hero, winning a medal a week.'

'My father's dead,' said Paul.

'Dead in *my* war?' said the Daisy-woman.

'Don't be an idiot, darling,' said Molly.

'But he did fight in the Great War,' said Paul. 'He got the MC.'

'Ah!' said the Daisy-woman.

She took a pace forward and raised her arms as if she was going to hug Paul. He only just managed not to edge away. If he hadn't already decided she was mad—madder if anything than Mad Molly—he would have thought she was drunk. Mrs Fison, who was married to Uncle Charles's gamekeeper, sometimes got drunk and when she did had that kind of look, dazed, miserable, not quite sure whether she was dreaming or waking. Paul was concentrating on the Daisy-woman, apprehensive about the hug and puzzled by her behaving like Mrs Fison, so he didn't notice when Mad Molly changed.

'Look at me, Paul,' she said.

Her voice still had the bubble of amusement in it, but the note of mockery was gone, and a sort of excitement or happiness had come in. When he turned to face her she was bending forward, staring at him in a way that compelled him to stare back, to study her without shyness, just as she was studying him. She was not, he saw, terribly old—nothing like as old as the Grannies, for instance, no, only a few years older than Mummy. The reason he'd thought she was old was the way she usually held herself, very straight and proud, like a granny. But her hair wasn't white, just pale blonde with a bit of grey. She wore a lot of powdery make-up but it wasn't there to hide wrinkles. Her face was a bit like a cat's with its small pointy chin and neat mouth, and then the wide, high cheek-bones and those round blue eyes . . .

'Your father was a lieutenant and then a captain in the Warwickshires,' she said. 'He got his MC when he was wounded at Bixschoote. His name was Cyril but everybody called him Rogue. He could juggle five wine glasses at a time.'

'I . . . I didn't know about the glasses,' said Paul.

'Can't you see the likeness, darling?' said Mad Molly. 'This is Rogue Rogers's son! Don't you remember that night at the *Vache Ivré* when he tried to dance the can-can with his leg still in plaster and we had to smuggle him back into hospital at four in the morning?'

The wind sighed among the chestnut leaves. The Daisy-woman shook her head slowly from side to side. Tears began to stream from her eyes.

'Don't bother about her, Paul,' said Mad Molly. 'Tell me, have you any brothers and sisters?'

'There's a new baby, but she's only a step.'

'So·sensible of your mother to marry again,' said Mad Molly, the mocking note back now. 'How did poor Rogue come to die so young? He was as strong as a horse when we were looking after him.'

'It was in an aeroplane,' said Paul. 'When I was five. My godfather was going to start an airline in South America and Daddy went out to help him. They had a new aeroplane and it was bigger than the one my godfather was used to. He let the wing touch the ground just after they'd taken off. Daddy was in the plane with him. They were trying it out.'

'What rotten luck!'

'Much better than dying in bed,' said the Daisy-woman.

'You're going to come to tea with me on Sunday,' said Mad Molly.

'I'm afraid we're only supposed . . .'

'Piffle. Annette will arrange it with Mr Smith. She can bring you down.'

'But . . .'

'Goodbye, Paul. Remember, if you don't come I shall turn up in church the Sunday after and kiss you in front of the whole school.'

Mad Molly spun away and strode off down the path. The Daisy-woman, still weeping, stumped after her. Paul stood among the soaring rough-barked tree trunks with his mouth opening and closing, as if it were still trying to say words that hadn't come. In any case he had no idea what they would, or could, have been.

6

Dobbs's response was the last I could have expected.

Admittedly I was apprehensive about the material I had sent him, because it had so little to do with his own interests. For different reasons I wasn't all that happy with it myself, though I had evolved what seemed to me the beginnings of a promising plot. I won't go into the details, but it was to do with spying on the naval base at Exmouth, via the officers who came to Molly's Sunday teas; its only significance to this book is that I could have persuaded myself that such an implausible farrago made sense; I would, I now see, have been satisfied with almost anything that allowed me to write about Paul, and Molly, and the Captain, and the deer. But at the same time I was aware that these elements, in particular the deer, were beginning to put the book out of balance.

Yet the deer were vital. I knew that at an irrational level. They were the key. For example, if Dobbs at our first meeting had had time to ask me how I'd come to meet Molly, I would have said something like, 'Oh, I was out for a walk in the park and I ran across her and we got talking and it turned out she'd known my father.' But the details of the incident, which apart from a few turns of phrase I believe I have now recalled exactly, were wholly lost to me until in describing Paul's almost-ambush of the deer by the lake I once again saw in my mind's eye the way that particular hind leaped with shock at the sight of me. Instantly I also remembered—re-lived would be a better word—the parallel leap of shock inside my own torso when Molly crept up behind me. I found this process of rediscovery immensely absorbing. I wanted to go on with it, even though I knew that in practical terms it wasn't either what I should be doing to earn my living or what Dobbs had asked for. I quite expected some form of reproof from him. But certainly not a telephone call at 3 a.m.

I loathe being telephoned in the small hours. It always gives me a headache next day. One wakes with such a pulse of alarm, one feels the need to rush and crash through the dark to stop the wretched thing clanging away, waking the whole house. One's sure it's a wrong number but at the same time aware that something semi-appalling may be about to be sprung on one—one of the children being picked up for drunk driving, for instance, or worse. One's sleep-metabolism is disrupted by the rush of daytime biochemicals, especially if it's a wrong number after all, and there's nothing one can do to absorb the loosened energies.

I picked up the phone and enunciated my own number.

'Rogers?' said a voice, a stranger still, at the far end.

'Yes.'

'Dobbs here.'

'Oh . . . Can it wait till morning?'

'I'd rather not, if you don't mind. I take it I've got you out of bed.'

'Yes.'

'I'm sorry about that. I picked up your stuff because I thought it might help me sleep.'

'We have our uses.'

Dobbs didn't respond either to my meaning or tone. He sounded, if anything, angrier than I was.

'This figure you refer to as the Captain,' he said. 'I take it that he is not a complete invention?'

'The Captain?'

I was bewildered. I suppose I must have known what Dobbs was talking about, but the passages had been clearly marked (or rather left unmarked) by me as not really concerning him and therefore to be read as fiction.

'Captain Smith,' he said. 'One of the new masters in your latest instalment.'

'Oh. Both pretty well factual so far, I think. But . . .'

'What? Oh, I see. No, I'm not concerned with the other

57

chap. But the Captain in fact both looked and spoke as you have described?'

'Best I could do.'

'I take it that his name was in fact Smith?'

'Yes.'

'May I ask you to think carefully about my next question? You have him say something about speaking nine languages, and you follow that up with a phrase . . .'

' "I am wanted by the police of five countries." '

'That's it.'

'Well?'

'Did he in fact use those words?'

'Often.'

'Oh, God!'

I had stopped being angry. The semi-appalling seemed to have happened, but not, this time, to me. I waited.

'You tell me you don't know much about Steen,' said Dobbs at last.

'Not really.'

'You are aware that he was bisexual?'

'I'd gathered that much.'

'I have a theory on which I have put considerable weight in my book. It is well known that Steen had far more affairs with women than with men, but was at the same time more casual about his heterosexual relationships. My belief is that he had adapted for his own purposes the ethos of the warrior tribes among whom he spent his early manhood. Those years were crucial to him in a number of ways. Among these was the fact that the tribesmen were polygamists who regarded their wives as property whose primary function was to breed more warriors. The man's most important social relationship tended to be with an apprentice warrior, and this expressed itself in a kind of ritualised homosexuality. You follow me?'

'Not a very fashionable attitude these days.'

'No. Following this line I argue that the really important people in Steen's life were about five young men.'

58

'What about Molly Benison?'

'I wish I knew. That's why I'm going through these bloody trunks. But let me finish. I have a reasonable amount of material on the first four of these men, but almost nothing on the fifth. Steen was sharing an apartment with him in Paris in 1921, but did not go about with him as he had with the others. His existence, or presence at a gathering, is occasionally reported. All I have is a phrase in a letter of Rose Macaulay's that he had the head of a Roman emperor on the body of a ballet dancer, and a remark by Reginald Turner that he was a sinister figure who used to talk about being wanted by the police of three countries. His name was Richard Smith.'

'Good lord!'

'You see why I felt the necessity to ring you at this unpleasant hour?'

'Yes. Hold on a tick while I get my dressing-gown.'

Dobbs had evidently been waiting impatiently enough to be speaking before I got the receiver to my ear.

'. . . what this means?'

'Smith knew Molly Benison?'

'What? Oh, I expect he did. They were in Paris . . .'

'I don't think they gave much sign of it when they met.'

'You saw them together?'

'Two or three times, I suppose. At Molly's Sunday teas. She once asked me . . .'

'I'd prefer to put her on one side for the moment, if you'll forgive me. The question is, is it the same man?'

'Looks like it. Tell me, did Steen prefer his young men to be beautiful?'

'Within reason.'

'I'd be prepared to concede that Captain Smith was striking, but . . . Oh, I don't know. Twenty years younger and without that incredible moustache . . .'

'You agree it is probably the same man?'

'As a working hypothesis.'

'All right. Let's go on from there. I need to know everything I can about Smith, not simply to tidy things up. I believe him to have been much more than the last major figure in Steen's emotional life, in fact to have had a crucial influence on him which may explain Steen's dramatic shift of viewpoint to pessimism about the human condition in his last two books. These are in my opinion Steen's crowning achievement, really important contributions to our under-standing of ourselves and of the world. Their bleakness of outlook after a lifetime of preaching a gospel of hope has never been adequately accounted for. The change coincides with the end of his affair with Smith.'

'Yes, I see.'

'I suppose there's a possibility the man's still alive. He would have to be a little over eighty. Do you know how long he stayed at St Aidan's?'

'I think he left the same term I did—end of summer '41.'

'Not very hopeful, I'll try the teachers' agencies. It might be worth putting an ad in *The Times*. You don't remember anyone saying anything about how old Smith got hold of him. Smith . . . oh, bugger it . . .'

'Shall we call Mr Smith The Man and Captain Smith the Captain?'

'That'll do for the moment. I want to draw your attention to the coincidence here. I don't say it's impossible that two people involved in Steen's life in Paris in 1921 should turn up by chance in the same backwater in Devon, but it seems to me more likely that the later arrival came there on purpose.'

'I don't . . .'

'From what I know of The Man's habits he would have been perfectly happy to avoid agency fees by taking on a chance-come teacher who offered his services.'

'Well . . . you know, the Captain didn't give the slightest impression that he wanted to be there. He made out he despised the rest of the staff, didn't much like the boys and loathed the countryside. But he could be a bloody good teacher if he was interested in something. He could really put it over. I got my Eton Schol on a Greek epigram I translated right when all the others made a mess of it, because the Captain was nuts on the *Anthology*.'

'Snippets of homoerotics?'

'No sign of that, in practice. I was alone with him quite a bit.'

'Tastes too complex to be satisfied by fresh-faced boys, do you think? The trouble is I don't know enough about him to begin to make a guess.'

'I doubt if I'm going to be much help to you. He hid himself, if you see what I mean. You never knew what he thought or felt, or even if he meant what he said.'

'So I'd gathered from your book.'

'Your idea is that he deliberately chose to come to Paddery to make contact with Molly Benison?'

'It seems to me possible.'

'Why on earth? Blackmail? She hadn't got a penny, and in any case she wouldn't have cared a hoot what anyone said about her.'

'Steen had a peculiar attitude to money. He made quite a bit and insisted on sensible business arrangements with his publishers, but as soon as he received any payments he spent the money or gave it away. He refused to invest or to save, on principle. I told you about his attitude to women and their purpose in the world. He left a number of bastards—I've traced five, for sure. He took very little interest in them, and could be extremely brutal with discarded mistresses. There was more than one suicide. But I can't find a case when he was less than at least tolerant of a woman who had borne him a child, and he always saw to it that they did have money. This was a consistent pattern for most of his adult life. Then, in 1922, he made a will—a highly uncharacteristic thing for him to do in any case. Under its terms the income from most of his books was to be divided between three named bene- ficiaries—mothers, though the will doesn't say so, of three of the five children I know about. The other two women had married reasonably well-to-do men. But the income from *To Live like the Jackal* . . .'

'I imagine that's where the real money was.'

'Sixty or seventy per cent over the years, I should think. He made a very odd arrangement indeed about that and *The Fanatics*, which until recently can hardly have earned twenty pounds a year. He set up a trust to receive the money and then disburse it according to instructions which were not to be disclosed. I've always thought this odd.'

'Rather Victorian.'

'More than that, completely out of keeping. Canny and secretive. Steen detested lawyers, and disliked secrets. For instance, he made no bones about naming the other three women . . .'

'Other?'

'So it turns out. I've just found who was getting the money from that trust. It happens that the agents who manage Steen's estate are the same as mine, and they let me take a look at the accounts. It was the simplest way for me to gauge the continuing popularity of the various books. I did this some months ago, but I kept my notes. Last week I started on the second trunk of Molly Benison's papers and found a bundle of bank statements from the early Thirties. The larger payments are actually detailed in the statements as coming from the trust Steen had set up, and coincide with the amounts accruing from the two books. You follow?'

'Yes. Yes, of course. But, for God's sake, she never had a penny! She kept telling us so! She kept saying that was why she had to live in a borrowed greenhouse!'

'You've lost me.'

'It was a rather grand conservatory, actually, with a gardener's cottage attached. She'd asked Lord Orne—you know, the chap who actually owned Paddery—if she could live there, and . . .'

'She asked him if she might go there for a short rest in the spring of 1939. I've found a letter from him dated March 1942, reminding her of the fact and asking if she was yet sufficiently rested. She wasn't paying any rent, you know.'

'But that was the idea of Annette having a job.'

'Lost me again.'

'Annette Penoyre. She lived with Molly. Molly got her the job teaching Freshers so that she could help pay the rent.'

'Typical.'

'Of whom?'

'Smith. Benison. Everybody, I dare say. Shall we call it a night? I'm keeping you up.'

'I shan't sleep now. It's up to you. I don't want Steen barging into my book, but it looks to me as though Molly must have meant more to him than the other women you describe, and that's why he left her the money. Is there any chance she had a child by him?'

'No. She lived so publicly. I've been into that. As far as I can make out there wasn't a moment in the period when she wasn't in some gossip column or other once a week. On the other hand Steen certainly pursued her with some vehemence for a couple of years. They spent a lot of one summer sailing off southern Italy. It was a fair-sized boat and they kept it pretty full of friends who came and went. That's when Dufy did that picture of her lying naked on the fishing nets. I've a snapshot of her sitting on a deck with no clothes on which I think must date from that trip. I suppose she and Steen must sometimes have been left on their own, and letters and diaries from visitors seem to assume they were sleeping together pretty routinely. On the other hand there's a letter from Lawrence to David Garnett, bitchy even by his standards, which says Benison was deliberately keeping Steen in a permanent state of rut without letting him get anywhere. She did this with other men, both before and after. There are quite a few accounts of men trying to burst into her room at house-parties, or of her bursting out in the small hours because she'd let them in and then they wouldn't play the game by her rules.'

'Yes, I've read about that.'

'It was a game, literally, for her. She had a passion for party games—I suppose because she never had a chance to

63

play them as a child. I was reminded of this by your account of her creeping up behind you when you were hiding.'

'She was always extraordinarily kind to me after that.'

'Oh, yes. She was often forgiving would-be rapists.'

'You sound as though you don't much care for her.'

'I have developed a most unscholarly antipathy to the woman. I feel she is doing her damnedest to prevent me writing my book—leading me on and then turfing me out of the room.'

'I take it you don't think even Steen made it?'

'I think she died a virgin, in the technical sense.'

(According to literary-clique gossip Dobbs's own domestic arrangements had been far from simple. He had had a penchant for running off with his publishers' wives just when his books were in the proof stage. He had told me that he found it difficult to identify with the intuitive element in his subjects' work, but perhaps he was able to live imaginatively in Steen's shoes—bedroom slippers—at this point.)

'In that case, why did he leave her the money?'

'I wish I knew.'

'Trying to buy her favours?'

'If so, my whole conception of the man is mistaken and I might as well scrap my book.'

'Suppose he did, and she still wouldn't have him, he might have been too proud or too careless to scrap the arrangement.'

'It won't wash. She wasn't going to get the money till he died. And in any case, why do it like that? Why the secrecy?'

'Her idea?'

'You know her better than I do.'

'Apparently not, to judge by what you've just told me. She seems to have rather liked secrets. Your idea is that Smith, the Captain, may have known something?'

'Pure guesswork. I think he was an adventurer. I think Steen admired his outlook that the world was there for him to explore and exploit. Steen had been like that himself as a young man. I know that Smith left Paris in the early Twenties for the Far East, but there's no reason why Steen shouldn't have told him about his dealings with Mary Benison. One of my luckiest finds has been the diary of a young German with whom Steen was living in Trieste before the first war. Steen appears to have revealed his inmost thoughts to him, and to have expected a reciprocal openness, though he was notoriously reserved with the rest of the world.

'But suppose Smith goes knocking about the world for twenty years and then gets sucked or driven home by the outbreak of war. What is he to do? He appears to have been penniless. How is he to earn or cadge a living? Who does he know that has money? Assume that he has retained some interest in the people he met when he was with Steen. He makes enquires about Benison—no problem, with anyone so notorious. He might go down to Devon to see how the land lay, be told about the school evacuated to Paddery, write and offer his services. It would solve the difficulty of earning a living while he considered how to exploit whatever it was he knew about Benison.'

'The Man would have wanted references.'

'I wouldn't put Smith above forging them. Or he could explain that he had been abroad too long to be able to supply them. Tell me, Rogers, this moustache which so obsesses you—did it look like a recent growth?'

'It could have been, I suppose. Why?'

'Prevent Benison from recognising him.'

'You seem to be doing my work for me.'

'Not really. My primary interest is in Smith and his relationship with Steen, but as I happen to be working on the Benison papers at the moment and have just stumbled on this curious arrangement about the trust, I cannot but feel that Smith may also hold the clue to that. It is something that needs explanation, if only in a footnote.'

'Couldn't it be more straightforward? Suppose something happened between Smith and Steen . . .'

'That's what I think.'

'Yes. Well, suppose you're right, and it made Steen take a

65

gloomy view of things all of a sudden. Mightn't one of the results be that he decided it was time he made a will? He might have been genuinely fond of Molly, felt differently about her than his other women, known how feckless she was, set up this trust so that she'd always have a bit of income . . .'

'No. It sounds quite reasonable, apart from the secrecy, but . . .'

'That would be Molly's idea. As I say, she seems to have liked secrets.'

'What I am trying to tell you is that Steen had an almost mystical view of money as something evil. He was notoriously generous, but he used to say—quite genuinely, I believe—that he gave it away to get rid of it. The arrangements he made for his other mistresses were just enough to see that they didn't starve. You could say they were wages for bringing up his children. But to allow somebody to live comfortably on unearned income, somebody he loved . . .'

'Like old Pound batting on about *usuria*?'

'Exactly. Steen had been bitten by that bug. You'll just have to take it from me . . .'

'OK.'

'I can't tell you how tantalising all this is. The Benison business is only a minor part. There's a crucial gap to be filled. Smith, I've long believed, held the key, but he was lost beyond recall. And now you've brought him back from the dead but you can't tell me anything about him. Everybody agrees that the gap is there . . .'

'I thought Steen got dispirited because so many of his friends had been killed in the war and he came to the conclusion that there'd been no purpose in it.'

'That was his own line. One theory is that it was the effects of his illness, though the first physical symptoms didn't show up for another eighteen months. Then there are people like Baston who say that it was the failure of *The Fanatics*, and his own discovery that he was a phoney all along. And then there are the simple souls who say it was the result of his passion for Benison, though the next moment they're talking about how notoriously life-enhancing she was for everyone who met her . . .'

'I'd go along with that.'

'You see? Whether or not Smith was the cause, he was the only person likely to have known the answer. If you could remember anything, the smallest hint or clue, to reinforce my hypothesis . . .'

'Honestly, nothing I can remember offhand. It might come.'

Dobbs sighed, meaningfully, I thought.

'I'm sorry,' I said. 'I can see it must be very frustrating for you. But it does genuinely seem to be the case that the only way I can remember the sort of detail you're after is to try and fetch the whole past back, lock, stock and barrel. That stuff I sent you, about meeting Molly in the chestnut grove— I don't think I'd have remembered any of that if I hadn't been writing about the deer. I'd even forgotten how creepy poor Daisy O'Connell seemed. I got quite used to her later on.'

'I suppose so. How do you distinguish . . . Oh, forget it.'

'You sound a bit beat up.'

'I'm not too well, to be honest. Those tests turned out worse than I'd hoped. It looks like more bloody hospital.'

'Sorry about that.'

'I wanted to ask you about O'Connell anyway.'

'Do you feel up to it now?'

'How about you?'

'I'm game, I suppose, but I think it would be a mistake. If you're not in a positive hurry I'm much more likely to come up with the sort of thing you want by letting it float to the surface than by going dredging for it.'

'If you say so.'

'Shall we call it a day?'

'Oh, one stupid little thing. "Wanted by the police of five countries." In the Turner letter it's only three.'

'It was always five at Paddery. Perhaps he felt he'd had time to acquire a few more.'

'Fact or fiction, do you think?'

'We always assumed it was fiction.'

'Good night.'

'Good night.'

*

Inexplicably I had no headache next day, though I had lain awake the rest of the night brooding on the consequences of Dobbs's call. What he had told me about the Captain had been a jolt, because I had cast the Captain both as chief suspect and detective/unraveller of my plot. The idea that he had already known Molly but did not wish to be recognised by her was highly interesting. Molly's apparent involvement with my spy could be accounted for by grafting parts of Unity Mitford's story into her life. Suppose Captain Smith was working for British Intelligence, both before and during the war . . .

Nonsense, of course, even in the nonsense-world of spy-fiction, but it seemed to keep me happy, by hiding from me the knowledge that my book could no longer be written in that sort of shape at all. Though my plot might appear to be pulling itself together, Dobbs, by telling me what he had in that fatal conversation in the small hours, had introduced a disruptive factor into my imaginative processes, had slid the lens of hindsight between my eye and its object, throwing details into clearer focus but distorting shapes and relation-ships, and at the same time reflecting from the surface of the lens all sorts of matters which did not concern me, shadowy images of events that had happened on my side of the glass. Why, I actually knew the Dufy picture but hadn't realised it was a portrait of Molly. It is always called simply 'Nude on a Fishing-net'. I was able to refresh my memory because Dobbs sent me a postcard of it, saying, 'Sorry to do that to you. Hope you got back to sleep. I did not. Back to hospital Thursday. Send me some more, if you have it, especially about the O'Connell woman. Wrote French prose poems about dead soldiers. Lived with MB. My interest is that S detested her—I'd like to know why.'

I took this as an excuse to delay immediate back-tracking to weave in missing plot elements and settled down to provide Dobbs with more 'light hospital reading'.

7

Sundays were looked forward to, but then had to be got through. The apparent liberty of not having any classes or organised games could turn into a prison of boredom, especially on wet days. You got up half an hour later, and there were sausages for breakfast. At Brighton, in peacetime, it had been two sausages each, and if you ate quickly enough you got a third. At Paddery it was one, a blackish shell and porridgy innards scarcely flavoured with meat, but popular with the boys not for flavour or food-content but because of a kind of ritual agreement that sausages were a good thing.

After breakfast nobody (apart from one or two boys who might have a Sunday Drill) had anything compulsory to do till Church Parade, when the whole school assembled in front of the house and marched down East Drive to Paddery Combe Church, which lay just inside the park gates, close by the gardens. When they got back there was another hour of doing the same nothing-much (conkers, Monopoly, ping-pong, draughts or whatever the current craze dictated) until boys' dinner (shepherd's pie and cabbage, spotted dick with treacle). Then three-quarters of an hour writing home. School Walk, unless it was raining. Tea. Film show. Juniors to bed. Cocoa and biscuits for Seniors, carried into Big Space and consumed sitting round while The Man read aloud —usually Bulldog Drummond or the Saint, but sometimes *Greenmantle* or *The Island of Sheep*.

You were only allowed out on Visiting Days—one a term—and then only with your parents unless you had a letter from them saying you could go out with someone else. Paul had done nothing about Mad Molly's invitation, despite having it repeated in a note next morning—green ink, huge letters like a child's but more careless, thick, expensive paper. He had put it out of his mind, apart from the odd five minutes of vague fret, though he could easily have asked a duty master for advice, or gone to see The Man; but there was something about Mad Molly—her attitude, her practically saying that she expected him to break school rules for her sake—which made this seem impossibly difficult. Even by asking, he would have put himself, in the school's eyes, on her side. So it was a shock, and then an extraordinary relief, when The Man stopped him as he was coming out from Sunday breakfast and said, 'You haven't come to me for permission to tea out today, Rogue.'

'No, sir. I . . . I didn't think I could go.'

'Have you told Miss Benison?'

'No, sir . . . I don't know how, er, where she lives.'

'You'd better go, Rogue. She tells me she knew your father very well. Write a note and give it to Miss Penoyre before Church Parade.'

In fact Miss Penoyre came and found Paul. She put her head round the door of Schol while Paul was still trying to write his note, having made two boss-shots at it. He jumped to his feet.

'I'm looking for Rogers,' she said.

It seemed a peculiar thing to say, as he was the only person in the room; the school ran on the principle that masters were all-seeing, and the idea that after a fortnight Miss Penoyre mightn't know all the boys by name was difficult to accept for a moment.

'That's me,' he said.

'Oh, good. It's my Aunt Molly—Miss Benison, you know. She's got it into her head you're coming to tea today.'

'I'm just writing to say thank you.'

'I'll wait.'

She sat sideways into Twogood's desk on the other side of the aisle, landing with a slight thump. She was rumoured to be rather clumsy, but Freshers, with their own teacher and their own bedtime and dorm and so on, lived rather separate from the rest of the school, so there was little evidence for this apart from her once having fallen flat on her face on her way into prayers. She was so young—no older than some of the boys' big sisters—that Paul was actually aware of a difference between her and the real adults. And although she was not at all pretty, rather ugly if anything, with her round pale face and close-permed mousy hair, he felt an instinct to like her. She picked up one of Paul's discarded notes and read it.

'Oh, no,' she said, almost whispering. 'You must never try and impress Aunt Molly. She'll tease you about it till you wish the floor would open.'

'I didn't . . .'

'Do it her way, that's safest. As if you were talking. Just "Thank you very much. I'd love to come."'

'She wants to know if I like crumpets.'

'Do you?'

'A bit.'

'You don't want to start her off on a crumpet-eating competition, you see.'

'I suppose . . .'

'If she does start something like that,' said Miss Penoyre, frowning as she spoke, as though evolving a rule of life as much for her own use as for his, 'you mustn't wriggle out of it. She'll find a way of punishing you if you don't let her have her fun. The best thing is to try and win for a bit, and then let her beat you. But you mustn't let her see you're doing it on purpose. Get interrupted, or something. She'll probably cheat anyway. She does that when she has gin-drinking races with the Exmouth men. Hers comes out of a bottle which is mostly water. Just enough gin to make a smell if they're suspicious.'

*

Later in his life Paul used to look back on Molly's Sunday teas as if they were somehow a continuum, a timeless and eventless golden scene belonging to that age in his life. His memory of them was similar to his memory of the deer-stalks, which also blended into each other and became a long, delightful, lonely moment of roaming among the tawny bracken and gold-leafed trees. In the case of the deer-stalks the difficulty of telling one apart from another was understandable, but Molly's tea-parties must have been much more varied, because of the way Molly herself liked things to happen. She would probably have been bored stiff at Paul's Ideal Tea, had one actually occurred.

It would be clear dusk, for instance, with the sun going down through a changing range of pinks and golds to the west, the light catching and glinting in the curved glass of the conservatory dome, flooding in from so low an angle that it lit the underside of some of the huge, ribbed palm leaves and made the hairy collars of the palm trunks glow with russet highlights, like the pelts of some rough animal. Perhaps there was only one real evening like that, what with the shortening days, and the abrupt end of summertime, when the clocks went back, but in the mind's eye that magic light shone Sunday after Sunday on to the cosseted tropic foliage.

There would be people under the trees. The composition and activities of the tea-party must really have varied considerably, but in Paul's mind-picture there would be four or five men, with Molly, Daisy and Annette, sitting in a rough circle of creaking wicker chairs round the big black stove which stood at the centre of the conservatory where the main paths crossed. The doors of the stove would be open, the banked coke glowing like the sunset in the panes overhead, Paul on his stool toasting crumpets for everyone, his cheeks seeming to crackle with the close heat. It gave him a reason for being there, the only child among the adults. Molly never suggested he might bring a friend, nor would he have wanted to. The obvious apparent attraction of those Sunday teas —that they were not like school and more like home, like part of the holidays—did not apply. Home was nothing like this. Home was all right, but different too, because Molly was different. She changed things. She filled the conservatory with a feeling—a whole mixture of feelings—possibilities of wildness and freedom, a sense that there were no rules that mattered except not pretending to be anything but what you were—the glint and sparkle of life like the glitter of sunset in the dome, and like that too the sense of seeing everything strange and sideways—but above all the knowledge that it was just a fluke you were here at all, you couldn't have got here on purpose, not by asking, and now you had to make the most of it.

In the ideal picture Molly was vivid, but that didn't mean the other people were complete blurs. Mr Wither, for instance, was quite clearly there, though in fact he stopped coming somewhere about the middle of the term. Annette had originally brought him so that he could walk back with Paul. (The Man had agreed surprisingly easily when Molly had said she wanted Paul there every Sunday, but had insisted that he mustn't come back through the park alone.) Molly, though she shamelessly made use of Mr Wither's car and extra petrol to get him to ferry her around, also teased him cruelly about being ordinary, trapping him into revelations about the ordinariness of his family and his past life, and inventing desperately ordinary futures for him. She wasn't exactly snobbish about this, in any sense that Paul could grasp, but it was as if she had invented her own code of manners—not table-manners, but mind-manners—and poor Mr Wither kept getting it wrong and she wouldn't tell him why. He grinned and wriggled when she teased him, looking at her with a kind of amazement that anyone could be like she was, until she became suddenly exasperated with him and cried out, 'Oh, Christopher! You're too nice to live!'

Captain Smith came to two or three of the teas about midway through the term. He did not automatically figure in Paul's Ideal Tea, but if thought about he might be there, a definite presence; it was as if he had been able to retract his large personality into himself, no longer immediately signalling to any newcomer that here was somebody rather formidable; only when approached and spoken to might he have given that stranger a hint of the reserves of moral energy available to him. And there was another thing—the plants,

74

palms, hibiscuses, bougainvillaeas and all the tropical twiners and trailers seemed to suit him like a natural habitat; even his moustache ceased to be freakish and became just another exotic growth, so that he did not stand out (as he did up at the school, whether considered in the context of the milling boys or the gravely florid décor of Paddery itself) as something extraordinary.

He spoke little and without all his actorly boom, ate one crumpet with relish, listened with attention to all that was said to or around him, and left early after making ambassadorial farewells. At his first visit Molly tried to tease him but with no success, so that she turned with extra malice on poor Mr Wither. Next time she left him alone but Paul noticed her watching him half-sideways, and another time when he wasn't there asked Paul all about him—was he a good teacher, what did the boys make of him, why wasn't he in the army if he was really a captain, where had he been before St Aidan's—things like that. Paul only knew a few of the answers but Molly said, 'Never mind. I'll have him to supper one day and ask him myself. I'll choose a day when I'm cross with darling Daisy. Isn't it funny—he gives her the horrors? She's rather clever at things like that. It's a sort of second sight, very useful to a silly idiot like me, who trusts everyone. I always take her advice about tradesmen, whether they're trying to cheat me, you know. I wonder if there isn't something sinister about Captain Smith. He suits my jungle, doesn't he? Like a sleepy old tiger? I bet his cave is full of bones.'

Most or all of the other men would be officers from Exmouth, and sometimes one of them seemed to Paul to behave much more awkwardly than poor Mr Wither, but Molly didn't mind and just bossed him around like everybody else. She had invented a game like Grandmother's Footsteps, but much more complicated because players could approach 'Grandmother' up any of the four aisles that led towards the stove, and you could be penalised not merely for being seen moving but also for standing on the wrong part of the pattern of black and red tiles with which the aisles were paved. Molly usually won at the stalking-up part of the game, but the extraordinary performer was Daisy. When she was Grandmother it was almost impossible to get near her. She seemed to put herself in a sort of trance by the stove and to turn to and fro in a dazed way, but always at the deadly moment naming the victim in a leaden chant, solemn as a priest. She was like the creature in the nightmare, which will find you however you hide. She provided, in Paul's gold-haze image of those evenings, the necessary dark vibrations.

But almost as though she had been two separate people, he thought of Daisy as also doing something else. (No doubt, if he had chosen to, he could have summoned up yet more pictures—Daisy just sitting silent, nodding to herself, perhaps even weeping a little; or starting to tell one of the officers how important it was he should get killed as soon as possible, until Molly shut her up; or behaving like a perfectly ordinary dull old lady, only uglier than most.) One Sunday a new officer came, the squarest man Paul had ever seen, short and with vast broad shoulders. His square blue-white face was topped with very black coarse hair, and he had enormous hands with fingers so short that they looked more like toes. As soon as he was in the conservatory, before he had even taken off his greatcoat, he seized Molly's hands between these huge paws and held them, staring at her.

'You knew them all!' he said in a churchy whisper.

'Oh yes,' she said. 'You must be the one who wants to talk about books and paintings.'

'I do! I do!'

'Come and meet Daisy,' she said. 'I'm no use to you. I could tell you till the cows come home about writers being sick in my kitchen and painters trying to get into bed with me, but really I never opened a book and I still think a Brownie makes a better picture than anything.'

The officer's face changed ridiculously. Perhaps because it was so big it looked somehow like a child's, a child who has had all its sweets taken away. Molly laughed.

'Daisy O'Connell,' she said, 'Dee-Dee.'

Again the huge mask changed, this time to amazement. Delighted with her game, Molly led the man across to where Daisy was sitting. Paul's composite picture of her at the Sunday teas included this quite different woman, crouched forward in her chair, spouting a mixture of French and English—neither language making much sense to Paul— moving her hands about with fierce little clutching gestures as though the ideas she was discussing were objects which she could somehow catch and hold, while the sailor sat on his folded greatcoat at her feet and gazed up into her face like an adoring mastiff.

'Look at them, Paul,' whispered Molly. 'Aren't intellectuals a scream? I wonder if you'll turn out like that, or are you a bit too cautious? You have to go the whole hog, you see, the utter whole hog.'

Paul looked. Molly often talked to him about her guests, as if the teas were a sort of people-lesson. Sometimes she did it out loud, in order to tease and embarrass, but more often for him alone. But not really for him, for her. He was somebody she could say things to without interfering with the game she was playing—like one of the Sunday games back at the school, Monopoly or something, but with the people performing both as players and pieces. Because Paul was not grown up he was outside the game.

He couldn't see the sailor's face, only the devotion expressed in the curve of the spine and the crane of the immense neck. But Daisy faced him directly, and he could see how different she was, not just in her attitude and animation but in her physical appearance. She was even paler than usual, and her face was more lined and twitchy, but at the same time less blurred. Of course she was never really blurred, like an out-of-focus photograph, but that was the impression she usually gave, somehow smudgy and difficult to recognise. Now you felt you would have known her anywhere, not just for her ugliness. She looked a bit like Mrs Fison sometimes did after what Fison used to describe as 'one of her evenings'.

77

Daisy glanced up and said something to Molly in French, a question. Molly answered in the same language and Daisy returned to the sailor.

'I wish I could talk French like that,' said Paul.

'You'll have to fall in love with a French girl,' said Molly. 'I'll find you one—you're twelve now—in four years' time would be perfect. This stupid war *must* be over before then. Blonde or brunette?'

'Like you.'

'Oh no. That would be a great mistake. Not till you're thirty, at least. And then . . . then, Rogue, supposing you did find somebody like me . . .'

'I don't expect there is anyone.'

'Ten out of ten, Mr Rogers. But if there is, try not to take her seriously. You'll only get hurt. That's the best bit of advice I'll ever give you, so don't forget it.'

As usual Paul didn't know whether she meant what she said or was pulling his leg. It did not seem odd that Molly should be able to spare time to talk to him when there were all the adult guests she was supposed to keep happy. She always hopped about between conversations anyway, like a bird among bushes, but still Paul got more than his ration. The pattern began on his very first Sunday. He came in with Miss Penoyre, inquisitive at the steamy grove of the conservatory but expecting to be taken through into a proper room beyond, and there were half a dozen people sitting round this big black church-stove. Molly (still Miss Benison to him, then) jumped up.

'Hurrah!' she said. 'Listen everyone, I've been to the market and bought a crumpet-slave. His name's Rogue and his father was one of my darlingest friends. Come here, Rogue, and sit on this stool. Give your coat to Annette. Now, there are your crumpets and there's your fork, and here's a glove in case the fire's too hot for your hands. Oh, isn't this perfect! Sunday, and crumpets, and a slave to toast them!'

'I wish I'd brought my butter ration,' said somebody.

'Don't worry,' said Miss Benison. 'I've managed to wangle a bit extra from a sweet old farmer.'

The 'bit extra' was a bright yellow mound, three weeks' ration for a family at least. Paul was relieved to have something quite sensible to do, which he knew he could manage without making a fool of himself, but at the same time nervous about the potentialities of Miss Benison's madness. He almost dropped the fork when he was taking the first crumpet off it because she scraped her chair up close beside him and said, 'Lovely, I'll do the buttering.'

He muttered some kind of nothing as he passed the crumpet to her.

'Do you mind not having a father?' she said. 'I'm glad that funny headmaster of yours calls you Rogue, because it means I can too. Do you?'

'I've got a step now,' said Paul.

'Not the same thing. I adored mine when I saw him, although he was an appalling nuisance to everyone. We're different, us almost-orphans. Look at Annette. She never even saw hers.'

'I don't think I notice much. We don't seem to talk about our families when we're at school.'

'Isn't that funny? I thought about mine all the time, or rather I imagined families I might have belonged to. I had a very peculiar childhood.'

'Shall I do some of these browner than others?'

'Yes, if you like. They're best when the little black bits are just beginning to come, don't you think? But what about the holidays?'

'I've got three uncles. And I do like Duncan.'

'Shall I tell you about your father?'

Aunts in particular used to speak as though there was almost something wrong with Paul because he had no father, as though he needed special treatment rather in the same way Uncle Will had to have special food because of being gassed in the first war. Paul seldom actually thought about it, and when he did he managed to pretend to himself that he

79

was sorry, but at other times he had a vague unconscious idea that it might be quite a good thing, in some ways. A year ago, for instance, his school work had gone off the boil. He still came top of Midway but not as easily as before, so The Man couldn't really stop him going up into Schol. But The Man had written to Paul's mother saying that if he didn't pull himself together he was unlikely to reach any kind of scholarship standard. This was just after his mother had married Duncan, and poor Duncan had had the job of giving Paul a talking-to. It had not been comfortable for either of them, but Paul was aware that with a real father it would have been very much worse. A real father would have had so much more leverage, would have been able to squeeze and shove in ways Duncan couldn't . . . Paul assumed that he would have loved and admired his father, but at the same time he felt that the absence left a space for him to grow into, in his own way, at his own speed. Perhaps if his father had had more time at home, leaving Paul with more memories, it would have been different. Miss Benison's question was a surprise. It was not the kind of thing aunts suggested.

'It depends,' he said.

'It always does. Are you going to risk it?'

'Yes.'

'You're like him, you know. I arranged this on purpose so that I could see you sitting in front of that stove toasting crumpets. He used to sit like that in the hospital.'

'Were you a nurse?'

'They kept trying to send me home, but I got round them.'

'You must have looked after hundreds and hundreds.'

'Hundreds and hundreds. Lots of them became friends, but only a few were special friends, like your father. Of course he was English, and that helped. We had such a party when the news of his MC came through, too. It was one of the best nights in my life. He used to write to me for years. I've still got his letters—I just throw everything into a trunk and never look at it, but it's there. Lovely letters, such fun, just like the dear man. Isn't it extraordinary to think of somebody like that, with all that life in him, simply stopping—gone—because of a wing-tip getting a foot too close to the ground? And here you are instead, starting all over again.'

'Shall I do another one?'

'Oh yes. Don't stop till the crumpets run out.'

A man's voice laughed overhead.

'That sounds like your motto in life, Molly.'

'No, because they never will. I'll see to that.'

She rose to take the plate of buttered crumpets round but returned and went on talking about Paul's father. It gave Paul a curious sensation of only existing by accident, all this having happened long before his real parents had met—at a shooting-party near Bedford, his mother always said. Hearing about those old days was like hearing about an alternative world, in which there was not going to be a boy called Paul Rogers.

*

The ideal, run-together Sunday tea ended with Paul and Mr Wither walking across the park with the last light fading and a few stars out. The path through the chestnut grove would be strewn with shield-shaped golden leaves. Mr Wither could walk quite fast, using a sturdy walking-stick and lurching on to his deformed leg at each step, an effortful gait that caused him to pant after the first hundred yards and made conversation difficult. Paul walked with what he thought of as his hillman's stride beside him, using his gun as a staff. He always took it down to Sunday teas, just as he did on his deer-stalks, and in fact seldom thought of it as a gun. It had become a sort of talisman of his freedom to come and go as he wished. He kept it in a convenient slot between two stacks of lockers in the locker-room.

They would come up the last slope, Mr Wither panting, but also chuckling or muttering inaudibly and exuding a general sense of enjoyment of the world. Paddery would stand in front of them, a dark and silent cliff, all its black-out

81

in place, but the film show usually ended just about the time they let themselves in through the side door, and the night erupted with the racket of loosed boys.

8

How much of the foregoing is true, or even 'true'? I find it impossible to say. Take the question of Daisy O'Connell and the ultra-square sailor, about which Dobbs was to challenge me: that man existed, I know. He already figured in my vague picture of tea in the conservatory (a picture even less focused and organised than I have made Paul's appear). Thinking about him I summoned up a memory of Daisy talking with animation about books in a mixture of French and English, but looking more haggard and twitchy than usual. I believe that is also true, but admit that it might well be a product of my desire to create some sort of personality for her which I could then offer to Dobbs. With my after-knowledge I felt I could assume that the man she was talking to was one of the many conscript servicemen who compensated for the grind and desolation of their new life by stepping up whatever cultural interests they may previously have had—the audience for whom Connolly founded *Horizon*. The square sailor looked the part, so I put him in.

The details of conversation are obviously yet more dubious. Yes, Molly did say she would find me a French girl to fall in love with and I asked for someone like her, and yes, she said with apparent earnestness that I wasn't to try that till I was thirty and I would get hurt. And yes, I did get it into my head that she had nursed my father; but for that very reason it would be absurd of me to claim that her answer to my question was less direct than I'd taken it to be. To judge by Dobbs's next letter that may well have been the case, but at least at the rational level I had thought otherwise, and had made her answer as I had simply because most conversations tend to proceed with a good deal of clutch-slip.

Three explanations seem possible: coincidence; unconscious memory; imaginative truthfulness. As a writer who depends largely on his imagination, naturally I lean to the third. The imagination is a mechanism for producing worlds, and the more powerful it is the more coherent each world becomes. So, when you feed a few ingredients from the real world into the mechanism, your imaginary details and events must become coherent with reality, i.e. either true or 'true'. Again and again writers invent things which turn out to be facts. This is never the amazing coincidence it seems, merely a sign that the coherence-mechanism is functioning well. So I was cheered by the things Dobbs told me about Molly and Daisy. It made me feel that the machine was humming.

But if that was true of these sections of my novel it was not the case at all with the apparently straightforward work of going back and weaving in the material about plot and suspects which was supposed to turn my autobiographical ramblings into an orthodox whodunit. The machine groaned, hiccupped, juddered, stalled. The more purely invented the material, the less I was able to bring it into being. The two subsidiary masters—Floyd and Hutton—managed to stalk through a few unsatisfactory pages as just-visible ghosts of their real selves, but a quite fictional park ranger I needed simply refused to exist. Worse than that, he became a sort of nay-sayer. His unreality began to infect the areas surrounding the points at which he was supposed to put in an appearance. I was beginning to lose confidence in the whole idea (a vague but sinister sensation, analogous to the symptoms preliminary to the onset of flu) when Dobbs's letter came.

It was written in his own hand on paper from a ruled pad. I thought I detected a slight shakiness in the formation of the letters, and even if he had not said so I would have guessed from variations in size and spacing that it had been composed in several stages.

Dear Rogers,

Thank you very much for the latest instalment. I wish there had been more of it, but I cannot expect even you to produce at that sort of pace. Do you never get stuck or dry up?

As you will see from the address, I am back in hospital. Treatment this time. Less demeaning and uncomfortable than the tests, but involving drugs which make me sleep when I do not want to and then leave me lying awake when I— would give anything for oblivion.

I am apparently in for a longish stay and have a room of my own, so I have brought some work with me, to wit one of MB's trunks. This may seem madness, an unmanageable mess from a sick-bed, but it is intellectually undemanding —about what I am up to—and I must do something. Besides, I have become obsessed with the notion that the woman is deliberately preventing me from completing my book, and I will not be so used; though I fear that the deadline is now less likely to be Steen's centenary but (a less metaphorical use of the word) my own demise. Please do not pass this on. I am reading between the lines on my doctor's forehead and have told no one else; but having a need to tell someone I feel that you are sufficiently a stranger not to be seriously put out.

I am doing what I can to fight back. Against MB, I mean. I have taken the minor risk of sending the first two-thirds of the MS off for final typing.

Did you see my ad in *The Times* for Richard Smith? I must thank you for your further fleshing-out of him at the conservatory teas, though I hope you will forgive my saying he remains as much of an enigma as ever.

A propos, one of Lord Orne's complaints to MB was the cost of keeping the conservatory heated. Certainly by the time he wrote coke must have been hard to come by in sufficient quantities, but I suppose that if there was any of the stuff to spare anywhere in Devon it would somehow or other have found its way into MB's stove. Of course she had the gardener on her side; Orne refers to him as having said that the conservatory plants would have died in the winter of '41 (remember it? I was at Marlborough. We suffered) if MB had not contrived to get the fuel to keep the heating going. That was very much her style. She battened, but managed to make the relationship appear symbiotic.

That reminds me. She was never a nurse. I see you do not explicitly make her claim to have been. She worked for the same organisation as Gertrude Stein and Alice Toklas, something called the American Fund for French Wounded, run at the Paris end by a Mrs Lathrop. They took supplies to hospitals, blankets and bandages I suppose, but also a certain amount of creature comforts, with which MB no doubt made free. It was war work of a fairly privileged kind. Désirée O'Connell was the other member of her team, and it was through her that MB met Steen first, in 1918. The supplies for the celebration party when your father got his medal would no doubt have come out of the fund. I wonder what he was doing in a French hospital; but the fact that he was there would be a reason for the authorities to suggest that MB, as an Englishwoman, went in and chatted with him. I very much doubt that there were 'hundreds and hundreds' of similar cases.

I find your account of O'Connell quite interesting. Either you have a better memory than you claim or you know more than you are letting on. I think I told you she was a poet, and rumoured to be the illegitimate child by a Frenchwoman of some Irish *littérateur*. She wrote exclusively in French, prose poems derived from the Imagist idiom, quite untranslatable. Rimbaud's *Illuminations* are the closest well-known approximation I can give you. She signed her work 'D.D.' Did you know this, really? It would not have been pronounced quite as you have spelt it.

She was always notoriously plain. Many accounts mention the contrast between her and MB, but having made the point the writer of course concentrates on MB. Only the crasser observers considered the relationship to have been lesbian.

The general opinion was that MB did not want to live alone and kept O'Connell around for the contrast, and as an *entrée* into intellectual circles. Furthermore, O'Connell had a small income and MB nothing. I will come back to this.

O'Connell's importance to me is that she was apparently in love with Steen. Steen did not reciprocate. Far from it. He disliked her in a manner I cannot parallel elsewhere in his life, though he had a good number of enemies. He acknowledged that she had a certain talent, but thought she was putting it to obnoxious ends. I think I told you that he went to great lengths to prevent her coming on the yachting trip with MB (or did I? These drugs make me hazy about such things). Some of her later poems appear to be about her love for Steen, but they are too hermetic to be any use to a biographer.

You imply but do not directly state that by the time you knew her she was a thoroughgoing alcoholic. Do I also detect an implication that for the interview with the odd-shaped naval gentleman she had deliberately sobered up enough to be able to converse at an intelligent level? There is a casual reference in a letter from Apollinaire to Braque about seeing her very drunk and throwing bottles at people 'as usual'. Her drinking was Steen's overt reason for refusing to have her on the yacht; he said he didn't want to keep fishing her out of the sea; but as I say he disliked her anyway, and no doubt felt he would have more chance with MB if she were not around. She must have had the constitution of an ox if she was still drinking on that scale seventeen years later. Where, incidentally, did she get the stuff in wartime?

On the other hand it throws a new light on MB that she was prepared to take on such a liability over so long a period. I doubt that O'Connell's small private income would by now have been a sufficient incentive, even with MB's preference for what she called 'living off the land' (really no more than the shameless exaction of hospitality from anyone who could offer it).

All this is academic, for my purposes. My professional

interest in the pair stops abruptly in the early Twenties, when Steen seems to have come to the conclusion that he was never going to make it with MB, and simply left Paris. He must have had the first indications of his illness about then; he was seeing specialists by the end of '23. And whatever it was that happened between him and Smith came at this time. Then he shut himself up and wrote his last two books.

Did I tell you how good I think they are? I take it you have not read them, but if you find yourself near a reputable library read the fourth chapter of *Honey from the Rock*. The book is a discussion of the place of the Jews in Western civilisation, but typically Steen didn't use the subject in order to contribute to the so-called Jewish Question, but as a sort of paradigm of all human behaviour. Chapter Four will make your hair stand on end if you read it remembering that it was written eighteen years before Buchenwald.

How did he come to look at the world with those eyes? That's what I want to know. He might have written as good a book ten years earlier, but it would have been quite different. I feel as though I had written six hundred pages as mere preparations to answer that question, and now I can't do it. God, let Smith see my ad and answer it. Supposing he's still alive.

Meanwhile I amuse myself with irrelevant speculations about the household you encountered. For instance, do you know the real status of the girl you call Annette Penoyre? You make her refer to MB as 'Aunt Molly'. This of course might mean anything in the usage of that class and period and certainly cannot be said to imply, let alone prove, an exact relationship. I think MB can have had no kin closer than second cousins. The one really worthwhile thing to come so far out of these intolerable trunks is a letter from Steen in which he makes it clear that the opening sequence of *The Fanatics* is closely based on MB's own experience. You have her saying she had a very peculiar childhood, and that was certainly the case. Collating bits of Nineties gossip with Steen's novel, I think the facts were probably these:

The parents were an appalling couple, the father a sort of gentleman horse-coper, the mother vapid, disorganised, sexually accessible to a remarkable degree but in a manner so unlikely to arouse genuine passion that she was more tolerated than you would have expected. They moved in the very outermost fringe of the circle that surrounded the Prince of Wales (E. VII-to-be), sometimes living together, sometimes apart. One silly hack has 'proved' that the Prince was MB's father, but this cannot be true; she would have been better treated. Neither parent had brothers or sisters but both were related by cousinage to a number of county families, and they developed a technique of blackmailing these with a threat that they themselves would come to stay unless the family in question took care of the child for a while. In the end the Gore-Phillipses took her on most of the time, on the understanding that they did not have to bring her up with their own brood. As a result MB spent most of her childhood in large Gore-Phillips houses where the family were not at the time residing; Eaton Square in August; their Scottish hunting-lodge in mid-winter; and so on. *The Fanatics* opens with the hero as a child wandering round a huge fake-Gothic castle on the west coast of Scotland, with the main rooms dark because the shutters stay closed all winter, but with blazing coal fires in the grates in an effort to keep the damp out, and for company two old couples who speak little but Gaelic. It is one of those passages which speak, which have an imaginative charge not accounted for by the material described. Steen's letter says, 'I have stolen your childhood. I must have it for the novel. It is what I have been looking for these past eight years.' I am fairly certain that he is talking about this opening sequence.

As a matter of fact I was working on this very question when I had to come in here. *The Fanatics* is not, even in the eyes of devotees, a success, though Steen for a while regarded it as his major work. He had begun thinking about it before the war, but had then had his ideas drastically disrupted (I take it you *have* read *To Live like the Jackal*) and was unable to resume until something dislodged the inner log-jam. He seems to have persuaded himself that his encounter with MB had done the trick. This answers your question whether she did not mean something more to him than his other women, and I suppose I must concede that here the answer is yes. But her intrusion was, if anything, more disastrous than that of the Kaiser.

How did I get into a discussion of *The Fanatics*? These drugs do make one ramble. I shall have to get the medicos to put me on to something else before I tackle my final section. The maddening thing is that I have only eighty pages to go. If it weren't for this bloody woman! Forgive me, I know she meant a lot to you. Anyway, she cannot have been anybody's aunt. A trivial point, and irrelevant to you as you are writing fiction and could give her ninety nieces if you chose.

What else? I take it you put the remark about MB throwing all her papers into a trunk to tease me, but should I come across any of your father's letters I will put them aside for you, having (I'm afraid) read them myself. A curse of my method (of my temperament, really) is that I have to read every word. It has rarely proved worth while, but on those few occasions how worth while! Now that I feel myself to be in a hurry I am more conscious of the actual curse than the potential blessing.

I do wish *your* method (temperament?) had allowed you to deal more extensively with Captain Smith. I feel that MB is, typically, edging him out, though this is scarcely your fault as she is the focal point of your book. May I suggest that when you have finished a section you jot down for my use anything you can remember about him but which you have been unable to incorporate? Do not worry if it seems unlikely to be of use to me. I need straws to clutch at.

Later. This is all very rambling, I'm afraid. I have re-read your instalments so far and must tell you that I have done so with increasing doubts about the usefulness to me of what you are doing. How do even you know what is true and what is not? How do you distinguish between real memory and invention masquerading as memory? Of course in my trade I frequently have to extract fictional impurities from the accounts of supposedly reliable witnesses, where, for instance, somebody has added a bit of shaping embroidery to a favourite anecdote and has then retold it so often that he can no longer remember not seeing what his tongue has got into the habit of saying he saw. But with you I am trying to extract factual impurities from a fictional brew. Ironically this is what Baston claims the reader has to do with Steen's work. The *locus classicus*, on which Baston expends a whole chapter, is the back-from-the-dead episode in *To Live like the Jackal*.

Do you remember, Steen was attempting to follow von Lettow-Vorbek's retreat to Mahenge when he ran into a patrol and got laid out by a bullet across his scalp? His companions, four local tribesmen and his 'friend' Mshimbi, thought he was dead, dragged the body into the bush and buried him in a shallow grave before making off. But Steen came to, dug himself out and somehow or other found his way to their camp, where they all ran off, thinking he was his ghost. It's a bravura bit of writing, maintaining the actuality of detail and the sense of his own delirium in a marvellous balance. Baston makes hay with it, and concludes that there's hardly a word of truth in the whole thing. It is a key passage in his debunking exercise. My own view, if you are interested, is that it is true *enough*. Perhaps, as Baston says, Mshimbi and the others knew he wasn't dead and only heaped branches and a few clods of earth on him to hide him till it was safe to come back and collect him; and perhaps in that case they didn't go far away. Mshimbi told Baston as much, and that he was on his way back to the spot when he found Steen staggering along the trail. But Baston admits he paid him, and Mshimbi on that basis would have told him what he wanted to hear. Steen, I am sure, came to and found himself in what he believed to be a grave, dug himself out, followed and found his companions, somehow. By the time he came to write his book he saw himself, vivid as truth,

91

stepping in among them where they sat mourning in the moon-shadow under the bean-tree.

It may or may not have happened like that, and how shall we know? I am reconciled to leaving the question un-answered in Steen's case, but you are still here for me to question. When I feel stronger I may well challenge you, Baston-like, on a number of points. I hope you will bear with me.

Later. I have had a minor but extraordinary illumination which I must tell you about, because you have accidentally provoked it. It comes, I suppose, of thinking about Steen's back-from-the-dead adventure just after writing and think-ing about Désirée O'Connell. I believe her infatuation with him, and his consequent loathing of her, may be partially explained by the episode in East Africa. As far as one can make any definite sense of O'Connell's poems of the period, she was obsessed by dead men; she seems almost to have worked herself into a state of female necrophilia (clinically a somewhat rare complaint, I should imagine). Steen, by his own account, could be considered one of the living dead, and therefore providing her with an erotic stimulus scarcely available elsewhere. Steen, of course, took a quite different view of himself, as a creature brimming with excess life, and regarded the adventure as proof of that. The notion of being anyone's zombie would have disgusted him. I will get my secretary to bring me the D.D. poems next time she comes and see whether any of the later ones can be read in this sense. If only they weren't so ineluctably obscure.

I must get back to work; though, quite by accident, writing this rambling hodge-podge has turned out to be just that. I fear it will have been less use to you. To make up for wasting your time I will tell you that I have collated MB's bank statements for the late Thirties. Her finances improved considerably over the period. She spent less than half the income from Steen's trust and seems to have invested the remainder, quite cannily. The dividends (sources listed in statements in those days) rise steadily. There is a stray

92

statement from '51 by which time she is living wholly on dividends. The sizeable royalties from *To Live like the Jackal* must by then have been going elsewhere. (Where? Why? Another tormenting little mystery.) But when you knew her MB could certainly have afforded to pay Orne some rent. Or at least her share of the coke-bill!

I am in two minds whether to send this, for fear it will sound to you maudlin. I am not in fact awash with self-pity; anger is nearer the mark. Write to me soon. Don't forget, Smith is the one I want to know about. I have as much of MB as I can take.

Yours ever,
Simon Dobbs

Dobbs's hope that I would not be 'seriously put out' by the possibility of his death was badly off the mark. I was appalled. If anything, the slightness of our acquaintance made it worse. I have had friends die, both suddenly and predictably, and coped with my own reactions in the way one does. This was different, I think because it seemed to involve two deaths, that of Dobbs and of his book. Of course his publishers would get somebody else to finish it, but it wouldn't be the same thing—a zombie, to use his word. I sensed that if he did manage to get it done it was going to be very much what I have called a 'real' book, not just a contribution to knowledge, but a source of pleasure and enlightenment for readers long after most of the books of our day are forgotten. So, in a mysterious way, I felt it to be Steen's last chance too. It was very unlikely that another writer of Dobbs's calibre would take him up, especially if the uncompleted zombie work existed on the shelves, providing an apparently satisfactory Life.

It seemed to me that I had a duty to do my small best to help, even if it meant taking risks with my own creative processes. I would settle down to getting all the 'true' bits of my own book written before I did anything more about the 'fictional' bits. This *was* a risk, partly because I had never before tried to write a book except from beginning to end, and partly because in this case the coherence of the finished product was obviously going to depend on an organic inter-weaving of elements. If I let the 'truth' set too hard, the 'fiction' might never cohere to it. The result would be a mess like a cracked mayonnaise. Still, I felt I had a moral duty to give it a go.

Truth is the devil. Strange that I should be finding that out so late in life. External truth is bad enough, but internal truth is gone like a lizard on a sandbank, glimpsed at best as a sort of already-vanished motion. The preceding two paragraphs contain a kind of truth, but still they are humbug. Now it would be dishonest to delete them.

The real truth, if I dare use such a phrase, was that I knew my own book was going off the rails, that the 'fictional' element wouldn't wash, and that even the 'true' parts had suddenly become shaky as a result of what Dobbs kept telling me. The fact, for instance, that Molly was really quite well off. I remembered her as desperately poor (even the drinks tray was stocked because the officers used to turn up with at least one bottle between them) but managing by her own personality to shed round her a sense that her world was one of invaluable richness. This was an important factor in my picture of her, miraculous evidence for her creed that one could live one's life on one's own terms, rather than on the world's.

On the other hand I merely 'remembered' her referring to Daisy as Dee-Dee, and yet Dobbs told me I had got that almost right. My fictions at this level seemed truer than my facts. In deciding to do what Dobbs asked me I suppose that unconsciously I was hoping to provide myself with enough similar solid details to prop up my tottering structure. Mind you, I did not then acknowledge that it was already a near-ruin—I seemed to myself to be enjoying what I wrote.

Even less consciously (though I am now more painfully aware of my motives at that level) I must have wanted to get back to the deer. There was one particular half-afternoon in which I had actually been attacked by a stag in rut. This was an episode—like the finding of Mr Wither's body—which I could not be said ever to have forgotten but about which I never thought. It was like a known fact shut away in an unread book. I hadn't really even thought of using it in my novel. I suppose I told myself that it didn't fit in with my image of the deer, those tutelary spirits of what Paddery had meant to me, embodiments of wildness and freedom. But now, at a more sensible if less rational level, I was having to face the knowledge that wildness and freedom have their shadows in danger and suffering. The deer-like life that Molly could be said to have led must have caused a fair amount of chaos, and worse, in other people's lives. So in that sense the episode of my being attacked by the stag could be said to have become proper to the novel, though this was not the reason I gave myself for writing about it. Dobbs's request for more information about the Captain had triggered the memory, and only then had I realised that two longish encounters with him were linked with that afternoon, occasions on which he had momentarily exposed to my view glimpses of the creature that inhabited his baroque carapace.

I got the whole lot done in two stints of writing and sent it off to Dobbs. In my covering letter I tried to adopt the attitude to the news about his health which I thought he would prefer—friendly concern, faith in his book and so on. I tried not to let the curious near-hysteria I felt show through. I don't think I had any inkling myself why it mattered so much to me that Dobbs should not die before . . . not before he had finished his book, but I mine.

9

The summer holidays had almost finished the War, but not quite. It wasn't so easy now; on half holidays the single football pitch involved almost a third of the school; the colder air and damper ground made ambushes and lying in wait less attractive tactics; and though The Man had extended bounds eastward along the lake to include the chestnut grove, and had thus opened new battlegrounds, the variations on campaigns, ruses and assaults were becoming exhausted. The hay forts had of course gone long ago.

Still there were fairly frequent skirmishes among a few shrilling enthusiasts, and occasionally for no good reason the whole school found itself in the mood and hostilities were resumed in earnest. On one such morning Paul came out, having missed most of break because of doing extra maths with Clumper Wither, and looked down over the battlefield. He had his gun in his hand, having heard the racket while he was working with Clumper (one of the juniors had come back from the holidays with a ricochet-whine, much easier to make convincing than the initial crack of a shot). He stopped at the edge of the gravel, hoping to see where a sudden charge from the flank might have best effect. A tang hung in the air like the smell of smoke as the chill of an almost-winter night was eased away by the sun. Paul's skin, chilly too with long sitting, crawled and tingled in the mild warmth. The day was clear and golden, with trails of light mist along the surface of the lake. It was down there that the battle raged, over the yellow leaf-fall of the chestnut grove and in and out among the dark, ridged tree trunks. Too far for a charge, and in any case break must be almost over. Miss Penoyre, duty master this morning, was looking at her watch; the handbell stood on the gravel beside her. Paul let out a deliberately audible sigh, and she looked up.

'Boys have all the fun,' she said. She sounded angry about it.

'Can I ring the bell?'

'Three minutes. If I'd been a boy they'd have sent me away to school. You don't know how lucky you are.'

'You don't know how lucky you are having an aunt like Miss Benison. You should see mine.'

'I suppose so. I can remember laughing at her in my pram. But she's got other sides. Look how beastly she is to Chris. What's she got against him?'

Paul felt uncomfortable; there was a school rumour that Miss Penoyre and Mr Wither were in love, but this was just gossip, of no greater credibility than the long-standing myth of Matron's unrequited passion for Hoofer Hutton. (A whole series of Matrons had filled that role.) It seemed to Paul at the time that his discomfort arose from the way Miss Penoyre was using Christian names. That was all right down at the conservatory, not up here. . . . But there was more to it than that, a feeling that she was about to do or say something truly embarrassing, something more to do with Molly than Mr Wither, as if she was going to ask Paul to *choose* . . .

'She's only teasing,' he said.

'It's never "only" with her. The more she laughs, the more she means it.'

'Who means what?' said the deep voice of the Captain, close behind them. One of his characteristics, much noticed by the boys, was his silent walk. He seemed to float, with his small feet merely trailing along the ground, as though his bulging torso were gas-filled almost to the point of weightlessness.

'You were at Aunt Molly's,' said Miss Penoyre. 'You heard her getting at poor Chris. What's she got against him?'

The Captain gazed at her and nodded, accepting that Molly had so behaved.

'I will consider the matter,' he said

'Oh, please . . .'

He nodded again, closing the subject, and his dark, red-rimmed eyes turned towards Paul, moving slowly over him and coming to rest at last on the gun. Though his look expressed neither comment nor question Paul felt a need to explain.

'I thought there'd be time to have a go in the War, sir.'

'Some for fear of censure,' said the Captain. 'Some for love of slaughter, in imagination, learning later.'

He wasn't the sort of master you could please by making guesses at where a bit of poetry came from, and in any case Paul had no idea—wasn't even sure it was poetry at all—but at the same time made an intuitive leap to what the words were about, and then, naturally, couldn't resist showing that he'd done so.

'My father fought in the real war,' he said.

'I don't even know whether mine did or didn't,' said Miss Penoyre.

'Mine got the MC,' said Paul.

He put down his gun and reached for the bell, glancing up at Miss Penoyre for the signal to ring it. She wasn't looking at him but at the Captain, smiling as if he amused her. Paul realised with surprise that in spite of her being so much more like one of the boys than a master she wasn't afraid of the Captain. He might have been a large and friendly animal in her eyes, her guard-dog, only dangerous to other people.

'Of course your father fought,' said the Captain.

'Did you know him too, sir?' said Paul.

'Too?'

'Miss Benison did.'

You didn't normally interrupt the Captain, but he had seemed to Paul to speak of his father as if he was expecting some response, and then to react to Paul's question with surprise. Now, however, he turned his huge head straight towards Paul and stared at him with sudden ferocity, revealing more clearly than Paul had ever seen it before what the boys had somehow instinctively known from the first, that there was something inside him far more dangerous and alarming than the normal run of schoolmaster could command. Even Stocky at his worst could only make you miserable. This power to make your heart leap to your throat and sweat break out all over your skin was something different in kind. The effect only lasted an instant before the Captain turned away again.

'I think it is time for the bell, Miss Penoyre,' he said.

'Oh, yes. But you will think what to do about Aunt Molly and Chris, won't you?'

'Ring the bell, Rogers.'

Gripping the glossy mahogany handle Paul swung the bell from side to side at knee-level. You had to get the rhythm right, stopping each stroke abruptly so that the clapper really slammed into the brass. It was quite hard work. After a dozen swings Paul looked up for the signal that he could stop, but the Captain had taken Miss Penoyre by the elbow and was leading her away from the centre of clamour. He said something. She stared at him and put her other hand to her mouth. A pinkness tinged her sallow cheeks, making her look excited but a bit frightened. Paul did half a dozen more good swings and put the bell down. He watched the War end with a half-hearted charge out of the trees against enemies who had already turned their backs and were trailing up the hayfield. The landscape still seemed full of a ghostly ringing.

*

The Captain was late for Extra Greek. Paul waited in the dust-smelling little room where he did these extra lessons with increasing nervousness. It wasn't just that he knew he had somehow infuriated the Captain during break, in fact that didn't worry him much, because experience had shown that the Captain could change mood quite unpredictably. On the whole Paul enjoyed his private sessions with the Captain, though they were very different from the dolphin-like plunge and skim on which Clumper Wither led him through the kindly waters of mathematics. The Captain belonged to colder oceans, a creature too large for you to make out his whole shape, let alone his intentions. Still, Paul found it satisfactory to have such an adult pay sole attention to him for fifty minutes. It made him feel that he mattered.

Today, though, there was a school match. Paul hated these. Luckily, now that petrol was rationed, only the School XI went to away matches, but for home fixtures everyone paraded form by form in the courtyard and then the form heads marched them out to the football pitch, where they were expected to stand yelling 'Come on St Aidan's!' until the syllables were meaningless. After all that, the school nearly always lost. Because everyone in Schol except Paul, Higley and Dent ma. was either in the XI or a prae (praes looked after the visitors) Paul was due to head the procession, marching out his squad of two. The idea so disgusted him that on an impulse he had told Higley that he might be late, because of Extra Greek, and having done that he had made a sort of bet with himself: if the session with the Captain lasted long enough to cause him to miss the parade, he would go off on his own on a deer-stalk, and time it to reach the football pitch just before the match ended. Nobody was going to spot there was one less chanting boy there. It was this decision that made him nervous. Now that the Captain *was* late, and it seemed more and more of a possibility, he became steadily less sure that he could go through with it.

Coming in without explanation or apology, the Captain slid a sheet of paper on to the table Paul used as a desk. Instead of being one of the usual old Eton Schol papers it was four lines of Greek, written out in the Captain's tiny, print-like script with the meanings of the difficult words listed below. The last of these words was 'deer'.

'It concerns a battle, and the defeat of a king,' said the Captain, then turned and walked to the window where he stood, staring out. After ten minutes he came and looked over Paul's shoulder at three false starts. With a silver propelling pencil he drew a series of curving arrows across the poem, charting connections from word to word.

'Hello, they make a pattern,' said Paul.

'As the poet intended,' said the Captain and returned to the window. Helped by the arrows Paul sorted out a story which seemed to him to make a pointless kind of sense.

'Finished, sir.'

The Captain came over, his silent walk mildly ominous, and read the result.

'The average examiner might consider that a tolerable attempt,' he said. 'I find it offensive. Consider. These lines were written by a man of intelligence, a man with a purpose. That they have survived over two thousand years suggests that he succeeded in his purpose. What do you think he was trying to do?'

'Er . . . make fun of Philip, I suppose.'

'To wound him, to hurt his pride, to lessen his soldiers' trust in him. How?'

'Oh, he ran *like* a deer!'

There was a change of emphasis in the rumour of school life, that varying mutter that seemed permanently to emanate from Long Passage. It rose slightly as people stopped doing whatever they'd been up to and began to get ready for the match. Paul stared at the four lines of Greek. He could have asked about Philip, got the Captain going on Alexander . . . he was afraid to try.

'The note of gloating mockery is intentional,' said the Captain. 'This is a true war poem, much more so than something like *O Valiant Hearts*. The poet, a certain Alcaeus, understood about war. He saw the bodies sprawled among the rocks—unlike the hymnodist, whoever he may have been.'

'Arkwright, sir.'

'Your father would confirm what I say. I take it he met Miss Benison during the war, not after?'

'Yes, sir. She nursed him.'

'Did he tell you that?'

'He's dead, sir. When I was five.'

The Captain did not make any of the usual little mutters,

really mostly embarrassment at having mentioned the subject. But though the noise from Long Passage could now definitely be interpreted as a general movement away towards the locker-room for macs and caps (compulsory for match-watching) he made no move to end the session.

'How then did you discover your acquaintanceship with Miss Benison?' he said. 'Not through your mother, I imagine.'

As Paul started to explain he found his mind had made itself up. He would skip the match. Perhaps it was talking about Molly that did the trick, the knowledge that she would positively have approved of his rule-breaking. Perhaps it was the omen of being set a poem about deer to translate, perhaps something to do with the Captain's interest. At any rate he began deliberately to spin the story out, going into detail, even though this involved talking about the strangeness of Daisy's behaviour.

The Captain listened in silence, seeming to accept Paul's right to speak about another adult in that fashion. Indeed when Paul finished—by which time the school noises were trampings and squeaks of command, coming via the window and thinned with the lack of indoor resonances—he went further. For a moment the whole adult conspiracy—that huge unspoken pact whereby the shortcomings of adults, even such men as Herr Hitler, were never acknowledged, let alone discussed, in the presence of children—vanished.

'You believe Miss O'Connell is a madwoman?' asked the Captain.

'I don't know, sir. She's like . . . well, there's a woman I know at home who drinks too much . . .'

'Yes.'

'And I suppose that's why Miss Benison has to look after her.'

'So it would seem.'

'And Miss Penoyre helps.'

'Yes.'

'But I don't think she likes it.'

For a moment Paul thought he must have triggered off the same rage he'd inexplicably provoked that morning. The atmosphere, almost the smell, of the little room seemed to change, become heavy and musky. Then he realised that this time he was not the focus of this anger, if that was what it was.

'She dislikes looking after Miss O'Connell?' asked the Captain.

'No . . . I mean not that specially. I suppose I've only seen them with people about. It might be the way Miss Benison teases everyone.'

'Perhaps. I have suggested Mr Wither simply stops going to tea on Sunday.'

'She'll tease about that.'

'The roster for duty master changes at half term. Mr Wither can take over from me on Sunday evenings, beginning next Sunday. I tell you this because Miss Benison is certain to ask you about it. All you need say is that the roster has changed. There is no reason why she should be given an excuse to distress Miss Penoyre.'

'But she's very fond of her. She often says so.'

'No doubt. I understand that Mr Smith insists on your being accompanied back here on Sundays. Miss Penoyre will do that.'

'Thank you, sir.'

The Captain stood where he was, apparently brooding but making no move to go. It struck Paul that perhaps he too had spun the session out in order to avoid having to stand on the touch-line and watch boys galloping across muddy turf. If so, this was one of those conspiracies which you could spoil by letting on you knew it existed. Paul pretended to be studying the Greek poem. A picture came into his mind of a lot of men lying among hot black rocks, with blood all over their brass armour. Above them stood an enormous antlered stag.

From the distance, meaningless as the noise of waves on shingle, rose the cheering of boys. The match had begun. Without even a grunt of dismissal the Captain left the room.

*

Ten minutes later Paul leaned panting on his gun between two clumps of red-brown bracken. His whole skin crawled with nerves. He'd done it now. Paddery was out of sight behind the brow of the hill, and it was that moment, when the roof-top had vanished below the ridge, that had seemed to set the seal on Paul's rule-breaking. The danger of being spotted had been far greater when he was slipping out round the garage block and then scurrying down to the cover of Lake Wood, but now he was actually standing on what seemed to him forbidden territory. He ought not to be here. If he were found cutting the match, it would mean loss of praes' privs and at least one Sunday drill, but it wasn't that sort of punishment that produced this peculiar mixture of excitement and dread. It was the knowledge that The Man, in fact the whole adult world—Mummy and Duncan and everybody—everybody except Molly Benison—would think this wicked.

Well, he told himself again, he had done it now. He drew a long breath, let it out, and looked the forbidden territory over.

The day had lost the winter-warning smell which had been in the air that morning. The sun had gone too, leaving a soft grey day full of autumn odours. He was standing at the edge of a cupped plateau ringed on its further edge, about half a mile away, by the ditch and wall, with a belt of trees beyond them. There were no trees inside this bit of park and their absence made the space seem wilder and more desolate than other areas he had explored. He could see two groups of deer.

One lot was some three hundred yards away to his right, about a dozen grazing hinds, a few young stags, and a large male with branching antlers who stood on the skyline with its back to the others and from time to time stretched out its thick neck and bellowed. There was no cover in that direction, no hope of a stalk.

The second group was grazing on the further rise of the cup, quite close to the wall. That was much more promising. If he struck off slantwise between the two groups Paul could reach the ditch without getting too near to either of them, and then work his way back behind the bank and worm over the top. He started at once, but had not gone fifty yards when a fresh chance came up. The group he was after also had a boss-stag, which had been doing the same trick of bellowing at nothing but now moved stiffly away from its wives and began to roar even louder and more frequently. It was clear that it was roaring at something now, and looking along the obvious line Paul saw a third large stag approaching from the right, parallel to the wall. This animal now began to roar as it advanced. There was going to be a fight, something much too interesting to miss. Paul stopped to watch.

Now the boss-stag stood and waited, roaring its warning. The other stag came stiffly on, halting sometimes to roar back, until they faced each other a few feet apart. They lowered their antlers and waggled their heads from side to side, as if waiting for the right moment to charge. Beyond them the rest of the group grazed steadily, paying no attention at all. Paul realised that the two stags were too occupied with each other to notice him, and at the same time the commotion they were making provided him with a sort of cover from the rest of the herd. He gave up the idea of a flanking movement and walked directly forward.

The stags, in fact, didn't charge, but closed almost ginger-ly, adjusting their stance until their antlers locked. It was like a game with rules. 'The fight cannot commence until both contestants are comfortable.' Then they just shoved. There was a bit of sideways movement, but more as though they were searching for a better grip than trying to slip a horn-point past the other's guard. It wasn't nearly as exciting as Paul had hoped, but clumsy and a bit ridiculous.

He was near enough to hear the click and clack of antlers when the intruding stag lost its footing on one foreleg. The other bore down at once, forcing it to its knees and trying to bucket it backwards across the grass while it could neither get up nor disengage. Its neck twisted, and then it wrenched its antlers free, half-rolled away, got up and backed off. The other stag made no effort to attack it while it was down, but bellowed a warning as it rose. It shook its antlers, wheeled to one side and trotted off, unflurried. The winner roared again and started back towards its hinds.

At this point one of the hinds noticed Paul. He must have been about eighty yards from the main group, but only forty or so from the stag. The hind's head came up, its ears twitched and fixed (they always heard you before they saw you) and then the whole group was staring. The stag's head swung round too. Its antlers lowered. For a panic instant Paul thought it was going to charge. He stood still and raised his gun two-handed like a club. The stag stared at him a moment longer, then turned and followed its hinds, who were already racing away towards the skyline.

Paul stood, letting the fright die out of him. The stag had not looked at all clumsy or ridiculous when the big head had lowered in warning and the prongs of the antlers had faced directly towards him. Stupid, he told himself. Bad luck, too. But somehow, inwardly, he felt that the moment had been sent, was a sort of warning, because he was here at all.

As his shivers lessened he heard a change in the general sound of the afternoon, a distant steady murmur swelling up where before there had been silence. Of course, it was the school cheering. The silence had been half time, and now the match had begun again. Twenty-five minutes to go. He had better start back. The best way would be to circle to the left below the ridge, then down across the path to the gardens and up to the Temple, down again to East Drive and up through the trees to the latrines. (There were proper lavs in the school by now, but the latrines had been kept for boys who might want to 'go round the corner' during a game.) He'd have to leave his gun among the trees and come back for it later, so that it would look as if he was simply rejoining the spectators after a visit to the latrines.

He started off at the pace he thought of as 'the long, swinging stride of a man born to the hills', leaning well forward and using his gun as a staff. He now felt a need to reach the match well before it ended. Somehow that brief threat from the stag had spoilt the afternoon, making him for the moment just a frightened child, and not the self-reliant lone adventurer. He realised he had not really enjoyed himself. He had not been free. The mixture of excitement and dread, which twenty minutes ago had promised so much, seemed to have reacted and become a new emotional compound, almost self-disgust. It was as though he had let The Man down by rule-breaking, and also let Molly down by not enjoying the process. To yell for the school from the touch-line might help him get the taste of all that out of his mouth.

He had just re-crossed the ridge when he saw two figures coming out of the chestnut grove on the path towards the gardens. Luckily there was a small hollow close by, where a hole had once been dug or a tree torn up by its roots. He dropped into this and peered over the rim. It was Annette and the Captain, walking slowly along the path. Annette seemed upset. Indeed, though he was too far off to be sure, Paul thought she was crying. At one point she left the path in a staggering, clumsy run, halted and made a wide movement with her arms, a bit like one of Daisy's wilder gestures, hopeless and bewildered. The Captain followed her and put his arm round her shoulder before leading her back to the path. He seemed to be doing most of the talking. They went slowly, taking ages to reach the iron gate into the wood.

Though part of Paul's mind still buzzed with the fret of hurry, another part tried to make sense of what he saw. Suppose the school joke was true that Mr Wither was in love with Miss Penoyre, it would explain why Molly teased him in the particular way she did, and why Annette minded so much. Suppose that morning, while Paul had been ringing the bell, the Captain had taken her to one side and told her that he would help . . . she'd looked surprised and pleased . . . and now something must have gone wrong . . .

The moment it was safe Paul rose and free-wheeled down the slope, then fell back into his hillman's stride for the narrow, twisting track up to the Temple. He was still thinking about Annette and Clumper. He didn't particularly want to, but he couldn't help it. He felt he'd had enough of people being in love, at home, Mummy and Duncan, still whenever they thought no one was looking touching and stroking each other. You'd have thought, now that they'd had their baby . . . And now it was starting up here, at Paddery, with two other people he'd have liked to be ordinary friends with. And Annette was so young and plain, and Clumper was a cripple. How could they . . .

Paul had not been consciously trying to move stealthily, but the turf of the track was springy and soft, and a light breeze had got up to rustle the bracken, and the cheering from the match was nearer now; whatever the reason, just this once the deer did not hear him coming.

The last few yards up to the rim of the area below the Temple were steep, with step-like ridges in the turf. Paul came striding up these, eyes down to pick his footholds, and was out on the level before he was aware of the animals or they of him. The first he knew was a violent scatter of movement, that bellowing roar, and the inrush of the big stag.

He sprang back, caught a heel and sprawled. Somehow his gun was still in his hand and he slashed feebly sideways with it, so that it clattered against the oncoming antlers. The stag halted. Paul wriggled his knees under him and rose, still prodding forward with the gun, but the moment he began to back away the stag made another rush. He swung wildly and the gun banged against a prong, making his palms sting and almost loosing his hold, but stopping the stag again. He had to fend off two more such rushes as he backed across the arena before he felt beneath his heel the mound on which the Temple stood. He turned and scrambled up it, dodged behind a pillar and stood gasping. The stag had not followed him. It bellowed once more, shook its antlers from side to side and loped away after its hinds. Paul leaned shuddering against the bird-streaked statue. He felt sick with fright. His mind kept recreating for him the image of prongs, of black snarling lips, froth-streaked fur, a brown eye wide and crazy with rage. Though he was completely unhurt he felt as though he had been appallingly punished. It took him some while to pull himself together enough to run down the crunching gravel of the path to East Drive and up through the trees beyond. He reached the match just as it was ending, but nobody noticed his flush and panting because they were all so excited. It had, apparently, been a terrific match and St Aidan's had won 3–2.

*

Three or four days later Scammell came up to Paul while he was queuing in the kitchen passage for evening cocoa.

'Change of rules, praes' privs,' he said, snipping the words off in imitation of the officer who'd come and talked to the school a fortnight before about Dunkirk. 'Till end of term that temple thing out of bounds. Mustn't go within a hundred yards of any deer. They're out of bounds too.'

'Bound to be,' said Paul. 'Get anywhere near one and out it bounds.'

'Serious,' said Scammell. 'The Man says any nonsense and he'll keep praes inside Painted Trees. Told us at Praes' Moot just now. Said I was to see you knew.'

'What does?' said Dent ma.

'It's because of the rut. It makes them dangerous.'

'What's rut?' said Dent, because it amused him to watch Scammell blush.

'One of them had a go at Mr Floyd,' said Scammell. 'He was lucky to come out of it alive.'

*

Of course over the next two weeks when you met Mr Floyd you asked him to tell you about his adventure with the stag. Before he got tired of it he evolved a graphic story, full of scything antlers and snorting nostrils. It must have been the same animal that had attacked Paul, because Mr Floyd had gone to the Temple to take some measurements; he was planning to do scenes from *A Midsummer Night's Dream* in the arena next summer. The place had been empty when he started but the stag had turned up and charged at him. He told his tale slowly, with pauses for meditative puffs on his pipe. Details accumulated as the days went by, until it all became a bit of a joke and Paul was glad that he had been forced to keep his own adventure secret. But waking in the morning and hearing the distant roaring of the stags (which most of the boys had previously assumed to be only the way in which Devonshire cattle mooed) one still could experience a mild thrill at the idea of sharing the landscape with dangerous animals.

Curiously, the only person who from the first had not been impressed by Mr Floyd's story was Annette Penoyre. That very first Sunday, only a couple of days after the attack, she walked back to the school with Paul after tea in the conservatory. It would soon be dusk. They came out into the park and saw a group of hinds and a big stag close to the path. Paul hesitated.

'Come on,' she said.

'But Mr Floyd . . .'

She laughed.

'Just wave your arms at them and they'll run away,' she said.

She did, and they did.

10

How smells ambush one! The fact is notorious, but each time it happens it is a fresh shock. It must be the smell itself, not merely the thought of it, or reading or writing or talking about it. Will age ever undo the spell? Suppose on my death-bed I were presented with one of my personal trigger-odours . . .

I went to Richmond Park to look at red deer. I had no expectation of being able to smell them.

Though I had done what I intended, writing for Dobbs about the Captain and for myself about my encounter with the stag at the Temple, the stuff had not 'come' in the way I had hoped. As may be apparent to the careful reader (supposing I have one) I had had to fetch the material just presented with some labour. And yet it was all, I believed, true, even to the forgotten connection between the episodes. As evidence of this I may say that after writing it I had looked up the poem about Philip's defeat, and though the Greek meant even less to me now than it had when I was twelve, it was there. I don't believe I had ever thought about it in the interim. Its existence gave me confidence in the factuality of the Captain having set it to me that particular afternoon, and my then having gone on to talk to him about Molly and Daisy. But though I had got the stuff down, I was not happy about the feel of it. I thought it rang hollow. And worse, no fresh streams of memory were released.

No doubt my subconscious reason for going to Richmond was the hope that a more direct stimulus, a stronger dose of the deer-drug, would do the trick; at a rational level it was a simple piece of research; I had to go to London anyway, to attend another of those writers' committees, and passed the gates of Richmond Park. I had recently got three books about deer out of the library, but as well as reading them it seemed sense to fix an image of the animals clear in my eye and mind.

It was a lovely clear morning in mid-October and thus in mid-rut, and there the stags were, roaring; they were smaller of course than in my mind's eye, but still formidable to a grown man. Richmond is far tamer and the deer far more used to humans than was the case with Paddery, especially in wartime. It seemed unreal to be able to walk along a path within ten yards of a browsing stag and watch it raise its head to decide about me before going back to feeding, unalarmed. If after an hour of stalking at Paddery I had been able to get within that distance I would have been thrilled; and the animal the moment it had spotted me would have raced away with that peculiar gallop that seems to flow into great bounds over non-existent obstacles. I only saw this delightful spectacle once at Richmond, when some idiots let their dog yelp around after a group of deer.

The smell leapt at me when there wasn't a deer in sight. I was wandering under a stand of oaks when I caught the whiff, faint, and gone in a couple of seconds, though I walked around under the trees for a while, sniffing like a maniac. I cannot now describe it. Less musty than fox-smell, perhaps. Sweetish?

But I know it was the odour of a stag in rut because of what it did to me.

Re-reading, as I eventually had to do, all that I had written of my novel it became clear to me that I had really been writing it—had felt the initial excitement I had, the need—because subconsciously I had decided that the time had come on my inward calendar when I must face up to all that had happened to me on the night I had found Mr Wither's body. Perhaps the reader has perceived the odd reference to, and then shying away from, this event. As I've said, I had always known it had happened and had believed myself indifferent to it; indeed, the coroner at the inquest congratulated me on my cool-headedness. It never struck me until that morning in Richmond Park that perhaps the incident had been lying there, shut away in an attic of my mind, quietly infecting my whole life.

Why, for instance, had I forgotten to mention the smell of the animal that had attacked me below the Temple? It was more than a detail—it was central to the experience. Mr Floyd had noticed it too, and always put in a phrase about 'the bestial reek of the creature'. I was still apparently able to make the association between my adventure and my childhood distrust and bewilderment about adult sexuality, but this link seems to have been routed—as with brain-damaged patients—through unlikely channels in my mind. The natural channel, the one using my physical awareness of the stag's own potent sexuality, I had blanked right out. (I wonder whether my dislike of the kind of writer and man exemplified by Steen is another aspect of this. Also whether my own kind of writing—a mannered style employed in the invention of fantastical deaths—may not be my way of sublimating the object in the attic. I don't know. I don't think I wish to know.)

Until that morning I had told myself it would be obscene, or at least a kind of posthumous bad manners, for me to use the real details of Mr Wither's death in a novel. I was going to blow him up in his MG during an air raid on Exeter, the murderer faking one of those random bombs that were a feature of the war. A land-girl on one of my uncle's farms had been killed in just this manner while walking across an empty field. I had, I believed, been looking forward to the big scene of the raid, with Paul fire-watching on the roof at Paddery. But by the time I reached my committee that morning I discovered that for the past ten weeks my subconscious had been working with surprising persistence towards a different end.

And that discovery, together with the visit to Richmond, was going to do the trick. Not one, but three linked episodes had wavered up to the surface of the pool of memory. First the deer-cull, then Daisy going mad, then finding Mr Wither. They belonged to each other, not only in time-sequence and cause, but with a potent emotional linkage, so that I knew I could not write about finding the body without having cleared the other two out of the way.

The foregoing does not mean that I was proposing to write a lot of formless guff for my own gratification. I was still intending to produce a detective story, and in the same mental breath as that in which I had decided to describe Wither's death I had also decided that I would be able to use this as my crime in the novel. The moral repugnance of so doing seemed to vanish under the solvent of my own need as a writer. (I say 'seemed to' because this is not an argument to which I really subscribe. The artist is not let off anything for being an artist; he is under the same rules as the rest of us. But it is easy to persuade oneself otherwise while the fit is on one.)

As happens at such moments, all sorts of details seemed to quiver and replace themselves in satisfactory patterns. Even by that afternoon I found it hard to attend to the committee-work (Dobbs had sent formal regrets of inability to attend, with no explanation) because I kept thinking of things that would work.

For instance, Annette's laughter at the idea that stags could be dangerous. I had met an official in Richmond Park who said that in his opinion the chief danger came from people attempting to feed the animals, when a suddenly raised antler might cause serious injury; and though all of the books I had procured mentioned the occasional fatality, one of them actually had a footnote saying that the only confirmed misadventure of this sort was a death in a private park in Devon during the war. I saw how I could actually use this, as well as a host of other things, many of which I had included by accident, simply because I remembered them as true.

This process continued over several days, excitingly enough for me to be able to go back and work on the hitherto neglected plot-structure. I knew from experience that it would do no harm to let the scenes that followed from the deer-cull simmer for a while, vivid though they had now become in my mind.

While I was in the library getting the deer-books I had looked for a copy of *Honey from the Rock*, but all Steen's books were out on loan except *The Fanatics*, so I took that. I am an intolerant reader of other people's fiction, but I had what was for me a serious go at it, not giving up till page 100. The opening I thought truly impressive, despite my difficulty in preventing an image of Molly in childhood from inhabiting the shoes and clothes of the hero as he roamed the huge shuttered rooms with their blazing fires while the Atlantic gales threshed through the crenellations above. I was particularly struck by the one long paragraph about the billiard-room, the flames glinting off the teeth of the line of mounted lion-heads on the wall and the table sheeted as if for the autopsy of a giant. Of course Steen had put that in for the general symbolism of the book, but I wondered whether he had made it up or got it from something Molly had said. In a way it sounded more like Daisy's line.

If I were a more experienced novel-reader I might be able to say why the book then seemed to fall apart. There was something wrong, something I couldn't put my finger on. Steen was primarily a writer of ideas, with the ability to find big concrete images to express them. But here something seemed continually to intrude between idea and image. The mind revolved its mighty cogs; the imaginative pistons thumped; but somehow they never meshed to produce an output of power. I was increasingly depressed by the huge creative energy being so misused, frustrated, dribbling away, wasting itself page by page, as a life can be frustrated and wasted day by day. From the feel of the pages, incidentally, many previous readers must have given up at about the same point I did.

Dobbs's letter took longer to come than usual and then alarmed me by being a package, but most of its contents, though manuscript, were in an only vaguely familiar hand. His covering letter was comparatively brief.

Dear Rogers,

My secretary has been doing a preliminary sort of the next Benison trunk and has come up with the enclosed. I have read them, I'm afraid, but don't propose to make use of them. If I were writing a biography of MB (which God forbid) I would find them of definite value, but not irreplaceable. I tell you this to help you decide whether to keep or destroy them, or whatever. Naturally I would vote against destruction, but I have often felt that our cries of horror at the burning by relatives of a great man's papers, though in one sense justified, show a failure to grasp either the emotional values of a past period or the sense of shock which X may well feel on discovering that Y, so long lived with, loved, revered, was never really *known*.

I take it that your conversation with Miss Penoyre comes into the class you call guess-memory; I suppose she might recall being in her pram, say aged four. Even that does not necessarily prove that she and MB were already members of the same household. She could well be the child of friends, taken on for some reason at a later date, perhaps as late as the war.

I am of course wary of the way you 'remember' things when I ask you about them, and not till then. You may say that my question evoked the memory. The question arises from some fact in the real past, so a true memory must answer it. And I accept that there are several points where you have in effect answered questions which I had not yet asked.

I hope you will forgive my saying that I still find your portrait of Richard Smith disappointing for my purposes. This is not criticism of your handling of him for *your* purposes. You produce a picture of a man whose physical appearance is clear enough, but of whose inward landscape I can get no glimpse. I take it that this was his creation, not merely yours, i.e., a man in armour, his visor down against the world. There is no reason why, supposing I were well enough, I should not get on and deal with Steen's final years, the two last books, etc., leaving a few notional gaps in case anything new emerges about Richard Smith, but I find this very difficult to contemplate. It is ironic that I nearly decided not to trouble you in the first place about recollections of MB, and now I find you my life-line.

Did you see another piece in the *ST* Arts pages about the Steen film last Sunday? I'd better warn you that you may be approached about this. I had one of the scriptwriters here last week and told him about your memories of MB; he became a little excited. They have the problem of having hired a major star to play the part, and then not being able to give her enough to do. Now there is talk of making the whole thing her memories, a flashback from later in life, and as one major thread of the book is Steen's role as a disregarded prophet they might choose to set this during the Second World War. The idea of MB living in Orne's conservatory has obvious cinematic possibilities. If they do approach you, make sure you get some money out of them.

Returning to the idea of Smith as a man in armour. Do you think it possible that the rift with Steen hurt him as much as it hurt Steen? Can he still have been nursing some inward wound? Let me know.

My own intestinal campaign appears to be still at the phoney-war stage.

Yours ever,
Simon Dobbs

I was cheered by this letter—mainly of course by the possibility of getting a few pennies from heaven by way of film money—but also because it seemed to me to be written in a firmer hand than the previous one, and to have been composed at a sitting, though of course it was much shorter. I didn't know what to say about the Captain's 'inward wound'; the thought had not struck me, though I agreed with Dobbs's image of him as a man in armour; those deep-sunk eyes might well have been peering out at the world through a slit in some protective layer.

I turned reluctantly to the letters from my father. There were nineteen of them, starting in 1917 and finishing in 1932.

The first was a proposal of marriage and so were two of the later ones, the third proposal coming only a few months before my parents were married, indeed after I had imagined them to have become engaged. The general tone started extremely cheerful, witty and attractive. Even the declarations of love (the first two) were couched in a voice of amiable self-mockery. A darkening of tone, a note of time slipping away, abrading youth and ease, could be detected in the sequence before the first batch ended with the final proposal. There was a three-year gap, and then a stiff note of thanks for a glass spoon sent as a christening present for me, which I don't remember ever having seen; then another gap before the last two letters—one brief, dated late in 1931 and rather grimly apologising for a misunderstanding that seemed to have taken place in Paris a few days earlier. The nature of the incident was not deducible, but in the light of what Dobbs had told me about Molly perhaps guessable. Last of all came a long letter from South America, telling Molly how much she had meant to the writer and how often he thought of her. Though he had made a deliberate effort to recapture the champagne tone of earlier years—he wrote at length about remembered meetings and escapades—this seemed to me a very sad letter indeed. He told her of the plan to run an airline with my godfather (whom he simply called Ian, implying that Molly knew him too) but added something which my mother had never mentioned to me, and which I am not sure that she herself ever knew—that if the venture was a success she and I would go out and start a new life in South America. He made a joke about my becoming a little Spaniard. He died three days after the date on the letter.

I suppose I had really been waiting for Dobbs, using the excuse of getting my neglected plot-work sorted out, before I tackled the scenes which my visit to Richmond had startled me into recollecting. Or perhaps I had relapsed a bit into my old reluctance to confront them. Now, with my father's last letter to Molly echoing in my mind, I settled down to try and bring them out into daylight.

11

Two of the boys had already lost fathers during the fighting, both at Dunkirk. Three years later Greatrex was to be killed when his house on the Kent coast received a direct hit from a flying bomb. But the nearest St Aidan's as a corporate entity came to the physical disgustingness of war was the deer-cull that took place on the last Saturday of October 1940.

Breakfast began, as always, with the duty master saying grace. Then there was silence apart from the clicking of spoons on porridge bowls. You could get a drill-mark for even muttering to a neighbour to pass the milk. After five minutes The Man came in to read the fortnightly marks. Paul was still top of Schol, but by less than usual because he'd missed several batches of marks doing extra maths and classics. Higley was miles bottom of Schol and would be going back down to Midway. So on, through the school.

Then came notices. Fish got his soccer cap, which allowed everyone to cheer for ten seconds. There was the team against St Dominic's, but as it was an away match there was nothing about the drill for school support. Summertime was ending and the clocks would go back an hour at midnight. Sunday drills—Loader—second time this term. The Man looked up from his papers but did not leave.

'Break will be in Big Space this morning,' he said. 'Nobody will go out before boys' dinner, for any reason. The deer are being culled today. This means that men are coming to shoot some of them. It has to be done. There are sick and weakling animals which must be removed if the health of the herd is to be maintained, and perhaps some healthy ones so that numbers do not get out of hand. They will also try to deal with the stag which attacked Mr Floyd by the Temple. I have arranged that as far as possible they will clear the area around the school this morning, but they are governed to some extent by the movements of the deer and we may have to stay indoors this afternoon as well. In any case all you will probably hear is a few shots. The shooting will be done as humanely as possible. It is necessary for the sake of the deer themselves, and the meat will be a useful addition to the food resources of the country.

'You may talk now.'

The usual metallic clamour of voices crashed out. The Schol table was never as noisy as, say 2a, but this morning everyone was calling congratulations to Fish, possibly overdoing it out of an urge to ignore poor Higley, scarlet-faced still and just not weeping.

'Look at Higger,' muttered Dent.

'A sick and weakling animal which must be removed if the health of Schol is to be maintained,' said Paul. He wished he hadn't, though Higley couldn't have heard. His tongue was always saying things like that, because they felt as if they were going to sound amusing, and they didn't. Dent frowned.

'I say,' said Twogood, 'we might get venison for boys' dinner tomorrow.'

'Not for a week, glue-head,' said Chinnock. 'Don't you know it's got to hang.'

'I think it's horrible,' said Higley suddenly. 'Don't you, Rogue?'

'I suppose they've got to do it,' said Paul. 'I mean, all the meat we eat has been killed by someone.'

'My aunt's a vegetarian,' said Twogood. 'She lets her corgi eat meat but my poor old uncle is stuck with cheese. They get extra cheese on the ration, though.'

Paul knew that Higley had only been making a fuss about the deer to hide the way he was almost weeping about going back down to Midway. There was a joke about the school cook having invented the vegetarian sausage; somebody made it again. Paul wondered why he wasn't shocked by the idea of men coming to shoot the deer, and decided that it was all right because of their wildness. It was the price of wildness. They lived their own lives, and being hunted was part of that. It would have been different if they were tame, coming up to you to feed out of your hand. But they were better wild. They could use that lovely racing run to try and escape from the guns—that belonged. Death among the bracken belonged too.

*

Nothing happened in the first half of the morning. Break in Big Space felt odd with the sun shining outside, not a cloud in the sky, the lake as still as a mirror; but it wasn't boring because the comics came on Saturday. Captain Zoom was back, and old Vultz; stupid, but you couldn't help reading them. Paul was doing so, perched sideways on one of the broad windowsills, when a van drove on to the gravel outside. 'R. & R. Boyce,' it said. 'Corn Chandlers. Exeter.' A fat man in green plus fours got out and opened the rear doors. Three more men emerged, carrying shot-guns. At this point Stocky came down the front steps and spoke to the man in green, who shouted at the driver and pointed. The van drove off towards the garage yard. As it went several more men with guns came in sight from that direction. They stood around on the gravel, pointing and arguing. One or two raised their guns to their shoulders and took imaginary aim down the slope. They looked a bit different from the shooting parties Paul had seen at Uncle Charles's, most of them fairly old and some not wearing proper shooting clothes, but grey flannel bags with the trouser-ends tucked into their socks. Some wore gumboots, a few breeches and leather gaiters. One of the men in gaiters also wore a bowler hat. Some of the tweeds were pretty loud.

'Hi, Dent,' said Paul. 'Come and look.'

Dent strolled over and gazed out of the window.

'Just a lot of tradesmen,' he said. 'Look at the way they're fooling around with their guns.'

'I suppose they'll be using buckshot.'

'Better had.'

'They're going to have to get jolly close.'

(Paul hadn't told anyone about his attempts to stalk the deer. Even Dent might be a prae next term, and then if Paul let on he'd pretty well have to tell The Man.)

'I expect they'll try and drive them,' said Dent. 'Like Dad does with the pheasants.'

*

Next class was maths with Clumper Wither. Paul had completely forgotten that the deer-cull was happening when he heard the first shots, one bang followed by another. The squeak of Clumper's chalk on the blackboard faltered and he looked towards the back window. Schol was at the south-west corner of Paddery on the second floor (there was really no first floor at this point because of the height of the ceiling in Big Space). The back window looked south over the lake and the side window out along West Drive. Clumper had started to write again when a whole volley of shots clattered out.

'Oh cripes!' said Chinnock. 'Come and see.'

You could, with Clumper. Chinnock had already twisted to kneel on the seat of his desk, his face close to the glass. His voice had expressed something more than ordinary lesson-interrupting interest. The other eight boys rushed to the back of the room. Paul, coming last, stood on the seat of what had been Higley's desk to look out over their heads.

More shots clattered as about fifty deer came streaming across the slope between the house and the lake, right to left, going faster than Paul had ever seen them move, the ones in front stretching into huge leaps as they went. Most of the others came on at the same marvellous pace, but there were knots and turbulences in the flow of movement, ugly disturb-ances in the beauty of wild speed, because . . .

The groups separated, and Paul understood. What he had seen was a wave of deer overtaking the stragglers from the previous wave, the ones that had set off the first volley of shots. Flat out they could cross the open grass in a few seconds, and they could overtake the stragglers because these had been hit, and now, as the unwounded animals swept clear of them, were left in the open, labouring painfully on. A hind only twenty yards from the gravel had her back leg broken, trailing and bloody. The blood came from a wound the size of a saucer, low on her rump. She fell, tried to rise, got her fore-quarters up, heaved, but could not force her hind leg to stand and so fell again. At once she started heaving forward and up, not understanding that it was no use. She did it again and again, heave and collapse, heave and collapse, getting a few inches further from the guns after each ghastly effort. It was too painful to watch. Paul climbed forward and stood on the writing-surface of Chinnock's desk to try and see where the men with guns were.

They had stationed themselves along the edge of the open space, using the trunks of the trees to conceal themselves until the deer had been driven in range. They must have decided this was a good place, because the beaters could then funnel the deer between the lake and the garage block which stretched out west from the main building, but it meant that they couldn't really fire until the deer were already past them, which is why so many animals were messily wounded in their hind legs. They went on shooting like this, though after the first two waves the driven deer must have known they were there and tried to swerve out from the funnel or break back between the beaters. Some of the shots seemed to be coming from along West Drive, which meant that there were guns out there to widen the mouth of the funnel. Two or three deer were in the lake, swimming for the far shore. A whole troop of them fled across the slope beyond. But small groups, or sometimes single animals, still came hurtling out from under the trees, pursued by shots; almost always the rhythm of limbs would falter and at least one of the group would drop behind, moving now at a stumble, but usually strong enough to reach the left-hand trees.

'My God!' said Clumper, from beside Paul in the aisle.

'I've got to stop this. Back to your desks, boys. Do set questions.'

Nobody paid any attention. He was clumping towards the door when Chinnock called out, 'It's all right, sir. Mr Smith's come.'

The Man strode into Paul's line of sight, heading purposefully across the gravel towards the fat man in green plus fours, who waved him away with angry gestures as soon as he reached the grass. The Man took no notice, but walked right up to the fat hunter and started to talk to him. Paul could hear that voice in his mind, The Man really angry, speaking his words slowly and not very loud, but completely flattening. Paul thought it might not work, used on an adult; and, yes, the fat hunter was arguing. The hunter next in line came up to join him. Stocky was crossing the gravel. The argument was going on, two against one, when Stocky arrived, but The Man said a few words and Stocky came hurrying back. The fat hunter put a whistle to his lips and blew. All the other men stopped shooting and came walking up the slope along the edge of the trees. Down by the lake three deer, almost as if they'd been waiting for their chance, raced into the open. Across the grass arena lay about twenty others, the ones near the guns quite still, but some of those which had got further struggling to rise or else twitching or threshing where they lay. The hind up by the gravel was still not dead.

The Man paid no attention when the hunters gathered round him, but spoke only to the fat one who had been in charge. Some of the others shouted, or pushed forward and tried to get into the argument. Stocky came trotting back, carrying The Man's Sam Browne with his first war revolver in the holster; all the school knew that belt because The Man often brought it along to show them when he was reading something like a Bulldog Drummond, where revolvers came in. The Man took it from Stocky and strapped it on.

Somehow that seemed to settle the argument. He was in charge now. He spoke to the whole group. They moved apart, obviously unhappy and angry, but still doing what he told them. He came walking across the grass along the line of the slope, but after a few paces glanced up at the school. He halted and with his left arm made a sweeping sideways gesture. Without words and at that distance the command was still unmistakable. Several other form-rooms looked south and, no doubt, at all the windows boys' faces could be seen, pale ovals behind the glass; masters with much more discipline than Clumper might have failed to keep their forms at their desks.

Paul was dipping his pen when he heard a different-sounding shot, just one. Shoes and chairs scraped on the floor.

'Better not,' said Clumper. 'He knows which window it is.'

'Sunday drills all round,' said Dent. 'What does, Chinners?'

'Killing the wounded ones with his revolver,' said Chinnock.

'Thank God,' said Clumper.

*

The Man said grace before boys' dinner which he usually only did on Sundays. He held up a hand to stop the kitchen staff taking plates round.

'Some of you may have seen that bad business this morning,' he said. 'It is the sort of thing which happens in wartime, when the men who know how to do it are away fighting the Hun. I have written to Lord Orne to tell him what happened. This afternoon nobody, and that includes praes, will go beyond the line of Painted Trees. The taxis will come for the First XI as arranged. Everybody else will join School Walk, with Mr Stuart and Captain Smith. Meanwhile the men who came this morning are going to search the park for wounded deer and dispose of them as humanely as possible. I shall stay to see that it is done properly, so Mr Hutton and Mr Stock will go with the taxis to St Dominic's. It is unlikely that the men will find all the deer they have injured, but because of petrol rationing and for other reasons, only four of them will be able to come back tomorrow, so we will have to take over. I will tell you about the arrangements for this later. I suggest that if you are writing letters you do not make too much fuss about what has happened. Thank you, gentlemen.'

*

Sunday morning was strange and beautiful. Only Freshers went to church. The rest of the school was organised into groups of three, each with a section of the park to search. A master, the Captain in Paul's case, was in charge of several such groups.

Paul and two 2b-ites, Hale and Porter ma., were given a curving valley to the north of West Drive, almost at the lodge gates, an area so far from the school that Paul had only crossed it once in his roamings. There was a copse on the left-hand slope. Paul decided to comb up the valley and back on the right, and then do the more difficult part with the copse.

There must have been a slight frost in the night. The air had that smell, like wet iron, but by ten, when they started along the hillside, the sun was warm on their backs. The ground was firm, but a little greasy on top. Only a few fronds in the bracken clumps retained their gold; the rest had subdued to a deadish brown. The boys moved along the slope about ten yards apart, keeping in line. Their instructions were to search any cover where a wounded deer might lie, but to keep clear of moving deer, study them, and report any that seemed to be injured.

Naturally all the deer were very wild and shy, and constantly on the move because of the search. Paul saw a troop of five scamper away north as he started up the valley; normally, seeing a human intruder at that distance, they would have left at a sedate and disdainful lope.

Paul had his gun and had made the other two find sticks. They stamped paths through the larger bracken-patches and poked into the depths on either side. It was a slow process.

After half an hour three hinds came running over the ridge, probably escaping searchers on the far side. One had a dark brown smear on its haunch and looked lame. They made for the copse. Porter found a last year's antler and insisted on carrying it with him.

Paul wasn't sure whether to search the copse or leave it and simply report that a wounded hind was hiding there, but as they approached it, searching the slope beyond, the three hinds broke cover and ran away south, so the problem was solved.

'We'll go very quiet and slow,' he said. 'We'll start at the outside, going round in a circle, and then we'll do the middle.'

Like all the woodlands in the park it was much more open under the trees than similar places which Paul knew at home. The trees were mostly oak and alder, and a few hollies. There were some nettle clumps at the edge, but no brambles—the deer seemed to keep them down. They were about half-way round when they heard a crash and a thump and a young stag broke out into the open ahead of them, racing away at a speed which showed there was nothing wrong with him. That seemed to be all, until as they passed a holly near the centre of the copse Paul heard Hale's voice from the other side, deliberately calm.

'Found one. Goner, I think.'

It was invisible until you lifted a branch of the holly aside, a young hind lying on its side on the pale spiny leaf-fall. There was a black wound on its flank and streaks of black along its underside and smears on the leaves. It must have bled quite a bit. Paul crawled in and tentatively touched a hoof, then gripped the thin leg beyond. The limb was stiff and the deer did not stir. He hauled the animal out into the open. They stood looking down at it, Paul thinking, *I have touched a deer. Pity it had to be dead.* Porter and Hale experimentally took a pair of legs each and lifted. They could get it clear of the ground, but only by raising their hands to shoulder level.

'Not like that,' said Paul.

Trying to work with the unhurried calm which he had found so impressive in certain adults, he untied the sling from his gun and used it to lash the animal's legs together, then poked the gun through under the knot.

'You take that end, Hale,' he said. 'Take your sweater off to make a pad on your shoulder.'

They had to keep in step, and rest quite often, and the back of the deer's head bumped and dragged on the grass all the way, but they got it down to the drive and found the Captain waiting. He gave them no praise, but sent them back at once to finish searching their section.

Paul worked along the final slope in a sort of sad exhilaration, something to do with being out of doors on a warm gold morning at the end of the year, something to do with having performed what he thought of as an adult task with competence, something to do with the idea of having at last touched a deer. He felt no sense of horror. The horror had been yesterday. In fact he felt as though he had been part of a kind of magic which was undoing the horror, making it come right, and that by finding the dead deer they were being allowed to know that their efforts were accepted. *It was the only way*, he said to himself. *I would never have touched a live one.*

*

After boys' dinner First XI and praes went off to be beaters. They wore scarlet XI shirts over their sweaters and carried red flags made by Matron. Four hunters had come back with proper rifles, and the idea was that they would now work systematically through the woods and copses where any more wounded deer might be lying and try to finish off as many as they could. They would start with Lake Wood and the copses on the east of the park. Meanwhile a party under the Captain would go along West Drive and collect the five dead deer that had been found on that side. There were two wounded and unable to move, but not yet dead; during dinner The Man went out with the boys who had found them to finish them off. When he heard about this Paul felt a wave of shock. So easily his deer might have been in that state, and then the morning would have been quite different in his mind, just ugly and pitiful, not sadly glorious.

The day changed for him, but only slowly. The first part of the afternoon was spent helping to carry two deer from a copse in the south-west corner of the park, well beyond the ruined chapel, back up to the drive. This was hard work, as they were full-grown animals and the ground was rough and boggy for some of the way. They used Paul's carrying system but it didn't work so well because the deer were heavier and longer in the leg, so that really it was a matter of four boys dragging them all the way. By the time he had done both trips Paul was muddy and exhausted. They piled the bodies on to the school's rubber-wheeled baggage trolley and hauled them back to the garages, where they added them to the pile from yesterday. There were twenty-three bodies in all, inside the furthest garage because of foxes—stags, hinds, yearlings, fawns, a bloody hillock of fur and horns and hooves and marbly dead eyes. The morning seemed ages away as Paul looked at them. A lorry was supposed to be coming to fetch them on Monday.

It was now nearly four, so he went and cleaned himself up, changed into his Sunday shirt, and started to look for Mr Wither to ask for permission to tea out and miss the film show. This was a formality, but The Man had told him to do it every Sunday so that the duty master knew where he was.

'Seen Clumper?' he asked Greatrex.

'Gone.'

'Gone?'

'Haven't you heard? Loader was there, looking for Clumper to report for his drill. Found him out in the hall in a bang-up bate, yelling at The Man in his Study about leaving and not coming back.'

'Clumper in a *bate*?'

Greatrex's large stodgy face was alive for once with the joy of gossip.

'Bang-up true,' he said. 'Saw him myself, off down East Drive in his buzzer, sixty m.p.h., luggage in the back seat.'

Paul treated the news as a standard school rumour, interesting but probably mistaken. Loader was most unlikely to have understood what he saw, let alone reported it right. That was the reason why the poor chap was always in trouble, breaking school rules not out of cussedness, but because he'd got them wrong.

'Oh well,' he said, 'bang goes my Eton Schol. Who's duty master?'

'Captain, I think.'

Paul couldn't find him at first, but then ran into him as he emerged into Long Passage from the green baize door that led to the entrance hall.

'Permish to tea out, sir?'

The Captain stared at him with his sullen, meditative gaze.

'No,' he said.

'But, sir . . .'

'No.'

'But . . .'

He managed to cut the sentence short. The Captain had dished out Sunday drills for the use of that one syllable. For a moment Paul thought this was about to happen to him, but then the Captain seemed to change his mind.

'The beaters are still out,' he said. 'You will wait till they return. You will then ask the head prefect whether the shooting has stopped. If it has, you may go.'

'Oh, thank you, sir.'

Paul went up to Schol to wait, filling in the time by scribbling his letter home.

*

Now, after the predictable let-down of the afternoon, the curve of the day suddenly plummeted. The sharp decline began at the moment Paul reached into the slot in the locker-room for his gun and found it wasn't there. This had happened before, old Dent teasing him by hiding it, always in some new place, but there wasn't time to play the game now and search. He was late for tea already. He didn't need it. It was only an old stake.

But as he trotted down the slope towards the lake path Paul felt strangely unprotected without it. He realised that for the first time since the maimed deer had threshed their lives away, he was crossing the actual ground where it had happened. For the last thirty hours or so he had achieved a mysterious, detached acceptance of the slaughter— probably The Man's doing, the way he had used his authority to stop the shooting and had thus asserted that the values St Aidan's stood for had weight in the real world—but now the ugliness of the incident reasserted itself. The horror was not over. Scammell had told Paul that the hunters had only managed to kill three more wounded deer. That couldn't be all. Somewhere in the chill beginnings of dusk there were deer wandering around the park with buckshot in them, the pellets burning into flesh, inward organs an oozing mess, pain like fire that would ease to a heavy ache when the wounds started to fester. And even the ones that were already dead, the ones The Man had shot to put out of their misery or whose wounds had been bad enough to kill them in an hour or two—their agony had been real, had happened, was part of the truth, could never be undone. When Paul had gripped the foreleg of the dead deer in the copse the touch of that stiff chill limb had been reassuring, had told him that the horror was over. But it wasn't. It was part of the world and always would be, because it was part of himself, inside him.

He ran faster. The change from summertime had lopped an hour from the afternoon, making his twenty-minute lateness seem much more. Night was not far off. There was going to be another frost. The nip of it was already in his nostrils. As he ran through the chestnut grove, though it was still light enough for him to see the far shore of the lake between the tree trunks, something like night fear gripped

131

him. It did not fully take shape. He was still running really because he was late for tea, but in an unformulated way it was as though the spirit of the park, the life that belonged there and expressed itself in the trees and the bracken and the lake, but most clearly in the deer, was gathering itself out of these vague elements and becoming a coherent thing, a being, which, when night came and it was fully formed, would stalk the park sniffing for a victim, a symbol of its vengeance for the senseless cruelty of the hunt. By the time he reached the iron gate Paul's pace, though nothing like a panic run, had become more urgent than a mere lope for lateness.

As the metal clanked behind him he slowed. He didn't want to arrive panting so that he couldn't speak. The un-imaged fear (like the knowledge that a dream is about to turn into a nightmare though nothing terrifying has yet occurred) left him. He was on safe ground, and at Molly's he would not only be safe, he would be happy again. She would restore by her presence the glow of the morning. That was really why he had been running so fast—to be with her. By the time he had passed the wooden door into the garden he was hardly panting at all.

There were lights in the conservatory, faint still in the pallor of day, but suggesting comfort and warmth behind the glass. The palm trees, lit from below, curved up in friendly silhouette. The conservatory looked like a bubble, with its own private world inside it. There was a boy in Midway called Colthurst whose uncle sent him science fiction magazines from America, and in one of these Paul had read a story about people travelling to and fro through the centuries in a sort of force-field, a bubble in time, which nothing could get into or out of because that would change the whole course of time. In the story they'd somehow managed to pick up a bacillus from the Black Death and brought it back into the future, but the writer had cheated in order to have a story at all. He should, Paul had thought, have somehow infected the future with an idea. But Molly's conservatory was like that bubble. Nothing that happened in the outside world could touch it. Her first words seemed to say this.

Paul found her sitting on his stool, toasting crumpets.

'Sorry I'm late,' he said. 'What are you going to do about the black-out?'

'It's all right. Nobody can see us here.'

'An aeroplane could.'

'Don't be absurd. Why should they bomb *me*?'

She got up and let Paul take the fork from her.

'I was hoping you'd bring me some lovely venison,' she said.

'I found a dead deer but I wasn't allowed to keep it.'

'Not my lucky day. Mr Boyce promised he'd let me have some—after all, it was my idea having a shoot in the first place—but then he rang up in a bit of a huff to say that your tiresome old Mr Smith had come out and stopped the hunt when they'd hardly begun. I'm going to write to Lord Orne and tell him.'

'Oh.'

'What do you mean, oh?'

'Well . . . you see, the men who came to do the shooting . . . some of them, anyway . . . they weren't . . . I mean, they did it all wrong. They weren't killing them cleanly because they were trying to shoot them from behind. Mr Smith was right to stop them. And he's written to Lord Orne already about it. I don't think . . .'

'You have to shoot some of them, Rogue. Every year.'

'Anyway, they killed quite a lot in the end—twenty-seven so far, I think, besides the ones that aren't dead yet.'

'Twenty-seven? What have they done with them?'

'They're up in one of the garages. A lorry's coming tomorrow.'

'Rogue, when I'm Queen of England you shall be my head spy. I am going to have a word or two with our Mr Boyce.'

Molly gave a sort of whining purr as she crouched looking at the stove, then rose to take the buttered crumpets round.

133

She did enjoy things so, Paul thought. She would have a-lovely time bullying Mr Boyce, and serve him right if he was the fat man in green. It was bad luck she'd been the one who really started the hunt, but she couldn't have been expected to know what a mess they'd make of it. And living in her bubble how could she understand the way the deer had suffered before they died?

There weren't enough people at tea to play Grandmother's Footsteps afterwards, just two officers from Exmouth besides Molly, Daisy and Annette. And in fact there was never really an afterwards because Molly trapped one of the sailors into a tea-drinking contest which dragged on through several fresh pots. Paul, remembering what Annette had said about the gin-contests, watched to see if she was cheating and decided yes. The teapot stood to keep warm on one of the fat iron hot-pipes that ran along the back wall by the drinks table. Molly took the cups over to the table to re-fill them, screening what she was doing with her body. When she came back she made a point of showing the sailor that her cup was full, but later she stood up to empty it, throwing her head back as if draining the last drops but standing so that it was difficult for him to see the real angle of her cup. No doubt he'd have enjoyed a gin-contest more. He was a stodgy, pale man, and after a bit Paul guessed he was longing to go round the corner.

So tea was not truly over before Daisy went mad. Molly was still dashing around, filling up cups, teasing everyone, making what they said sound funny just by laughing at it, or copying it in her clever way. Everybody seemed happy—or, in the case of Daisy and Annette, no unhappier than usual. Nothing made much difference to Daisy, but the more Molly sparkled, the jumpier Annette seemed to become. Paul saw her watching Molly like a cat which has been made to share a room with a boisterous puppy.

'Is she always like this?' whispered the officer who hadn't got trapped into the tea-drinking. He was new, and seemed to think that Molly was deliberately trying to amaze him.

'Oh yes,' said Paul, and had started to tell the story about Molly pushing the girls into the pond, when without any warning it began.

Daisy had stopped talking to the other officer about how lovely it was that he would soon be killed, and for some time had just been sitting nodding to herself as if she'd fallen asleep with her eyes open. When Molly brought her a fresh cup she'd gulp it down and go back to nodding. She was breathing so heavily that Paul wondered if she wasn't going to start snoring. Once, staying with Uncle Charles, he had gone to look for Fison and found Mrs Fison asleep in front of her stove, purple and snorting in her chair. It had been a ghastly moment. He had never told anyone. Now, not wishing to be reminded of it, he twisted round so that he didn't have to look at Daisy and could concentrate on toasting the last few crumpets. He didn't see her stand up. The first he knew was the sound of a chair falling over and a strange voice, deep as a man's, shouting, 'I want to play the game. I want to play the bloody game.'

'Not now, darling,' said Molly, not looking round from talking to Annette. 'There aren't enough of us.'

'That's your bloody fault,' shouted Daisy. 'You stopped them coming. You don't like being beaten, that's why you stopped them. You know I can beat . . .'

Molly had put the officer she'd been cheating on the pouffe, so that he should see her from as low an angle as possible. As Daisy now lurched towards him he half rose, but Daisy gave him a stiff-armed shove which caught him off-balance and sent him sprawling. His cup smashed on the tiles. She took another step and kicked him hard in the thigh. He cried, 'Ouch!' and tried to roll away, but she got another kick in. She was wearing heavy country shoes.

The other officer had stopped listening to Paul and was staring at Daisy with his mouth half open. As she turned towards him he sprang to his feet and backed away down the aisle between the palms. She was still holding her cup, and she threw it at him. It tinkled into bits beyond him. The sound seemed to excite her. She snatched up the shovel from the coke-hopper and charged at him.

'*Lâche, toi!*' she screamed. '*Va batter le boche, poltron!*'

'Oh, Daisy!' said Molly, putting her hands over her face and shaking with laughter. Daisy whirled the shovel back over her head and slung it at the officer as he ducked round behind the camellia bush at the corner of the aisle. The shovel sailed on and through the glass. Everybody except Daisy froze at the sound. Paul saw Molly staring, suddenly alert, in the exact pose of a deer the instant after it has spotted some danger.

'Daisy! Stop it!' she shouted in a voice Paul hadn't heard before. She dashed up the aisle.

Daisy was at the far end of it by now. On the shelf below the glass wall stood a row of ferns and other small plants in pots. She snatched one of these, found it too heavy to heft one-handed, so lifted it over her head and threw it like a footballer throwing in from touch. The officer must have dodged. At any rate the pot missed him and there was another crash of breakage and tinkle of falling glass.

When Molly was almost on her Daisy swung, seeming to know the instant the way she did when she was playing Grandmother's Footsteps. She charged, arms up and elbows bent to make a chest-high ram. Molly reeled off sideways, tripped on the kerb of the paving and fell among the bushes beneath a palm. Daisy stood still for an instant, so that for the first time since the madness had begun Paul could see her whole face. It was bright red, with purplish blotches, and contorted like a snarling dog's, all the muscles hard. By this time Annette was half-way up the aisle towards her and Molly was struggling free of the bushes. Daisy turned again, picked up another pot and simply slung it at the glass, shrieking in French as she did so. She got two more pots off before the women reached her and grabbed her arms. A moment later the officer she had started by throwing things at joined them and the struggle lurched out of sight behind the camellia.

All this while—though it had only been about twenty seconds—the officer Daisy had kicked had been standing by the stove, rubbing his bruise, muttering to himself. Paul looked at him for orders but the man looked away, so he swallowed and walked warily up the aisle. The fight surged back into view, Daisy still screaming. The officer had one arm held tight and Annette was struggling with the other, while Molly was behind with her own arm, thin and bony, locked round Daisy's throat. It may have been the tightness of this hold that made Daisy's face seem almost black now, and so contorted that it didn't even look like an animal's, more like the grimacing Indian demon that stood on the landing in Uncle Charles's house and which Paul had so dreaded having to make his way past when he was small, climbing the shadowy stairs to bed. The demon stared straight at him now, with live eyes. He was all it saw. It wanted him. Him.

'Rogue, door!' called Molly.

He jumped, pulled himself together, ran back to the stove, up the other aisle and round by the wall to the door in the corner that led to the cottage. He held it open, flattening himself against the wall to let the three of them drag and shove Daisy past him and on down the short corridor. They lurched out of sight through the open door of the little room Molly called her snug. He heard a crash. It sounded like a table being pushed over. He hesitated, hoping he couldn't be any help, realised that was true and blocked the sounds of struggle out by closing the door.

At once he was aware of a change, something badly wrong, even out in the conservatory. The air was usually still, warm, a bit too moist for comfort, but now an icy draught was fingering through it. On the curved glass wall straight in front of him were jagged dark shapes that did not glimmer with reflections of the lights inside. They were holes. The blackness of the night sky seemed thick and close, brimming level with the glass like water in the broken ice of a pond. Daisy had broken the bubble, and let the night in.

He went back to the stove and started to pick up cups and plates and gather them on to the tray—it was a way of being helpful without involving himself with the madwoman. The other officer seemed to have disappeared, but Paul heard the splash of a jet of water on the ground outside and realised what he was doing. He had carried the tray over to the drinks table and was nerving himself to open the door in order to take it through to the kitchen when Annette slipped quickly out, looking pale and hurried.

'Oh, Rogue,' she whispered. 'Quick. Can you do something for me?'

'Yes. Well . . . yes, of course.'

'You'll have to go back to school alone.'

'All right. Now?'

'Yes. Look, here's the torch. You can give it me . . . no, you'll have to bring it back here soon as you can.'

'All right.'

'But listen. On your way, go to the Temple. Chris is there. Tell him I can't come for at least an hour. But I'll come.'

'You know it's out of bounds.'

'Please, Rogue.'

'All right.'

'Please, please, don't tell anyone else.'

She had dropped her voice even further during the last exchanges. Paul hadn't heard the officer come back from outside, but now, perhaps attracted by the muttering, he came strolling round into sight.

'Anything I can do?' he said.

'It's all right. Really,' said Annette, picking up the tray.

'Brr,' he said. 'Bit of a draught through these holes now. Find some newspaper or something to bung them up, shall I?'

'Oh, yes, please.'

'Don't want the frost getting in, uh? You might remind Michael we're supposed to be back at base by nineteen hundred. If it's an emergency, of course, but well . . . there's a war on, as they keep telling us.'

'I'm sure we can manage. Hold the door for me, will you, Rogue?'

From down the corridor Paul could hear Daisy's voice, shouting but not screaming any more. There was a thud, a mild one. He found his coat, scarf and cap, said goodnight to the officer, and left.

*

Though it was almost pitch night he unconsciously chose to switch the torch off for the last few yards down among the trees. Only the clank of the gate behind him reminded him why he had done it. He stood still, just inside the park, letting his eyes get used to the dark.

It was really not too bad out in the open, although there was no moon, only the mass of frosty stars. He could see blacker blacknesses which were trees, and mottlings, which were clumps of bracken, and even—though perhaps only because he knew it so well—the line of the path. He could manage quite well without the torch here; there were no roots to trip over or branches or trunks to run into. He could just walk quietly along, not signalling his presence to any lurker or watcher. It was much better like that. Anyway, it was stupid to be afraid. Nothing could happen. It was only stories.

Yet he was afraid, so much so that he only realised when he saw the dark loom of the chestnut grove that he must have passed the track to the Temple. The thought of the darkness beneath the trees had halted him. He didn't want to go there. That was where he had first met Daisy. Going back by the Temple was a good excuse to himself, as well as being what Annette had asked.

Fear makes itself. It is like valley mist which, because it is there, chilling the still air, causes more mist to form. The idea that he was afraid, combined with the idea of Daisy, made Paul more afraid. However much he told himself he was behaving like a small child he felt fear closing round him, thickening, filling the park. It was as if the image of Daisy gave the mist something to collect around. Thinking of childishness only made it worse, bringing back those long self-nervings on the stairs in order to make the dash past the Indian statue or creepings back down to wait outside the door beyond which the adults were having their cocktails . . . Uncle Charles's voice, 'Honestly, Norah, you'd much better make him face it by himself. He's got to learn. He's not a baby any more.' Daisy with the statue's face. Wanting him.

The track was difficult to spot. It was only grass, after all, visible by day because of being shorter and greener than elsewhere. He started up in the wrong place and ran into a dead-end of bracken. Next time, to make sure, he switched the torch on for an instant. Yes, here . . .

But the instant was deadly. It showed them all where he was. As he started up the track the idea came back to him of the spirit of the park gathering itself for vengeance. In a way he had not been surprised by Daisy going mad, not just because she was so odd anyway, but because of a sort of feeling that it was somehow meant to happen. The park-demon hadn't got a body of its own. It had to take one over. It had got into Daisy and made her mad, yelling and screaming . . .

Why couldn't he hear her now? The night was very still. From far across the lake he had caught the quavering cry of an owl, but there was no noise from the gardens which were much closer. She'd got out! She was coming!

Without even willing himself to do so he switched on the torch again and swung round. The beam swept across silvery tussocks and brown bracken. Nothing there, and the night blind-black when he switched off. The sort of terror that only ought to come when you are fast asleep, dreaming, gripped him. It was no use running. It never was. Your legs wouldn't work. She was coming. He could hear. Hide, hide, though they always found you . . . Oh, if only I had brought my gun . . .

He was actually huddled down, sidling to crouch by a patch of bracken, when the terror went by like a breeze, leaving him gasping. Perhaps it was his own movement, real motion of muscles in a real world, that had done the trick. Perhaps it was the talismanic image of the gun. He stood straight and started up the hill again. Mr Wither was up at the Temple, of course. That made it a base—safe ground.

He managed now to keep moving, to stay just in control of himself, to keep at bay the sense of the real world losing its rules and going over to the unknown rules of the dark things. He put the torch in his pocket so that he shouldn't be tempted to switch it on again, and the nature of his longing for his gun became more sensible; just having it in his grip would help, not because it was magic. Really it could only shoot imaginary bullets and kill imaginary enemies, but if you used it to hit with, you could hurt someone. He was sure that the threat of it had saved him from the stag which had attacked him . . . Oh, perhaps that stag would be in the same place now, in the little arena between him and the Temple. If so, without the gun, what would he do?

It helped to think about a real danger. The deer had not been roaring nearly so much during the past couple of weeks, so it looked as though the rutting period must be almost over. In any case, if Mr Wither was there, he would probably have driven the stag away. He had a walking stick, too, though it wouldn't be as good as a gun. But just in case . . .

Paul had achieved what he felt was a sensible, daytime state of mind by the time he reached the short steep rise to the arena. He climbed it as silently as he could until his head was level with the rim, and peered over, half expecting to see the grass hummocked with sleeping shapes, and perhaps the stag itself standing sentinel, black against the stars. The space seemed empty, but was too dark really to be sure. On the mound beyond rose the Temple. Nothing moved between its pillars. Surely, if Mr Wither was there, expecting Annette, he would be standing quite clear, looking out towards the lake. But then, Annette had seemed to make a great secret of it, so perhaps Mr Wither would be careful not to show himself until he was sure who was coming.

He called softly, 'Mr Wither!'

Silence. No change of shape between the pillars. He was drawing breath to call again when the words became a creak in his throat as the waking nightmare surged back over him. Mr Wither wasn't there.

It had all been arranged to get *him* here! It was a trick, a trap! They'd driven him, the way the deer had been driven towards the guns. They were all in it, all three. Ever since that first moment in the chestnut grove . . . Daisy going mad, the fight, Annette coming whispering into the conservatory . . . Daisy went mad because she needed a death, it was time, the hour was on her. She used to weep because she knew she would go mad unless somebody died, and they hadn't. That was why she lived with Molly, to be looked after . . . But they were all in it together. They were there, waiting in the night, with a rope . . . trip him, snatch him, strip him, tie him naked to a pillar and Daisy, weeping, would slit his throat with a small knife while Annette watched expressionless and Molly laughed at the fun of it and the blood ran down over the white skin . . .

He started to run, not back down the path but away to the left, along a twisting deer-track through the bracken which would take him round to the path that led down to the drive. The drive, somehow, was now the first safe ground. If he could get down there . . . As in sleeping nightmares there was illusory hope—he knew the ground, and they didn't know he knew. They had expected him to go back down the path or on up to the Temple. They thought he'd need the torch . . . He stumbled, slithered on tussocks, almost tripped, but floundered on. The deer-track emerged on to the stone platform below the steps on the north side of the Temple. As he reached it he accelerated, unthinkingly, to take advantage of the better surface, but there was something large lying near the edge of the paving. He caught his foot and went sprawling.

He was scrambling up, scarcely even aware of his fall as more than another stumble, and turning for the path when something stopped him, a touch of the real world, outside the nightmare. The touch of whatever it was he had stumbled over against his bare knee. The memory of it remained down there, waiting to be summoned by his mind when it came out of the nightmare, the feel of solidity without hardness, stillness without cold. Nothing like some mound of turf or a log which someone might have left there; not even the hide of a dead deer. Cloth. A coat, with something inside it. Somebody.

Using all his sane will Paul just managed to force his hand into his pocket, take out the torch and switch it on.

Mr Wither lay face down below the steps with his stick beneath him and his broken spectacles beyond. He must have slipped and fallen. Paul shook his shoulder. No response. The cheek was warm, but . . . Paul's hand flinched back from a stickiness. In the torchlight the tips of his fingers were scarlet. He rose and crept round by the feet to the far side. There was blood on the flagstone. He crouched, keeping well clear, and shone the torch-beam level along the ground. Mr Wither's head was turned a little towards him so that he could see where the right eye ought to have been. There wasn't an eye there at all. Only mess.

Paul rose, drew a deep breath and let it out, blowing the shreds of nightmare away. He felt a sense of extraordinary relief, almost of happiness. It was as though Daisy had had her death and he was safe after all. Keeping his torch on he started to run down the path, but the crunch of leather on gravel seemed to fill the night and after the first few steps he swerved on to the soft turf at the side and went on down at a free-wheeling lope. Near the bottom a sudden glitter alarmed him, then he saw that it was the chrome headlight of Mr Wither's MG, parked beside the drive. Without stopping to look closer he turned up East Drive. With the slope against him now his lungs began to gasp the frosty air. The drive snaked, with the trees beyond it so planted that you didn't see the house until you had almost reached it. It stood as usual, a dark mass, but because somebody had left a chink in the black-out on the first floor it seemed less like an unwelcoming cliff than usual, more obviously a house, a home, safe ground. The chink of light vanished, but still there was that sense of ordered, ordinary life, with adults who would know what to do, who could take over. Paul raised his pace in a final spurt, wrenched open the door at the end of Long Passage and staggered blinking into the dusty light.

Total silence and emptiness. For half a heartbeat the nightmare brushed by, and then he told himself that he had come back early because of Daisy going mad, so the film show wasn't over yet. Slow footsteps descended what had been one of the servants' stairways to his right. He ran to meet them. The Captain was coming down—of course, he was duty master—he'd just been doing the rounds and seen that chink.

'Sir! Sir!'

The sunken red-rimmed eyes gazed darkly down.

'Mr Wither, sir! I found him! On the path by the Temple! I think he's dead!'

In proof Paul held out his red-smeared fingers. The Captain merely glanced at them, then back at Paul's face. He came another step down, and for a moment as he did so, though it may have been an effect of the dim stair-light, his eyes changed, the blackness of them becoming somehow hot in their red rims. He looked furious, dangerous.

'I know it's out of bounds,' Paul blurted, but . . .'

Then he realised he couldn't explain that Miss Penoyre had asked him. She had said he wasn't to tell anyone.

'I . . . I think the stag must have killed him,' he said.

The Captain nodded, took his watch from his waistcoat pocket and looked at it. Everything was suddenly ordinary again.

'The film will end in three minutes,' he said. 'Go and wait at the door. As soon as it is over, report to Mr Smith. Tell him I sent you and it is urgent, but do not say anything else until you are alone. Then tell him what you have told me. Say that I have gone to the Temple to confirm your story. Give me that torch.'

12

It may seem perverse of me, seeing that this book is being written and presumably read in the form of a detective story, to insist that the previous chapter was not in any way planned for that purpose. I had been aware, almost from the moment when the three incidents re-surfaced in my memory, that there were details in them which I could use in a fictional plot, but I did not emphasise them, let alone invent bits of plot-machinery, however tempting. My need was to get the events down on paper, as they had been.

Very hard work I found it, not for the reason I complained of before my visit to Richmond—that memory was beginning to run thin—but the opposite. Memory came in spate, more than my emotional sluices could handle. Just those three episodes, revolving like whirlpools on the turmoil, staying where they were, hardly moving despite the rush that created them, but going round and round and round.

One would have thought, for instance, that the inquest might have proved equally traumatic to a child, but I still remember almost nothing of it. Evidently the blanking-out process started almost at once. The point was brought home to me in all its strangeness by a press-cutting from the *Western Daily Mail* of 7 November, 1940. My wife's cousin lives near Exeter, and I had written to ask her to see if she could find something about the inquest in the Exeter reference library. I heard nothing for several weeks, and then the photostat came, taken on a poor machine and barely readable in its tiny, cramped wartime print.

'TRAGEDY OF LOVERS' TRYST,' it said. 'SCHOOL-MASTER KILLED BY STAG. PLAN TO ELOPE TO GRETNA.' The report had been hacked about by the sub-editor to cram it in. There was nothing about why Annette and Mr Wither had needed to elope, nothing about his row with The Man, or his having left the school. No mention, even, of Molly—an amazing omission, considering her notoriety over the twenty years before the war. The verdict was accidental death, with the rider that the stag should be found and destroyed. My name was given, and the coroner's praise for me reported. Incredibly unsatisfactory.

Gretna! Surely we must have known about that, in the school. The idea that Miss Penoyre was some sort of heiress, worth running off with before she could be made a Ward of Chancery, would have had a good deal of gossip value. And yet all I faintly recall is Molly coming to teach Freshers for a week and then Annette returning to duty—and even that may have happened at some other time.

Had anyone apart from myself and Molly even spotted that the pair were seriously in love? I assumed at the time Molly had, because of her behaviour towards Wither, and still thought I was right. The Captain seemed to have been told. Was it a peculiarly sudden deepening of a mutual attraction? Or had it been long brewing? They were both such shy people that they might well have managed to keep it quiet. In real life, as opposed to stories, people are secretive, and other people unnoticing. But still, Gretna Green? It had got into the papers, too. Surely we'd known?

Puzzling about this, and my own blanks of recollection, and the violence of such memories as did emerge, it struck me as possible that my own reaction to the whole set of events might have been warped by an earlier event which I've referred to several times but had always believed I'd simply taken in my stride—my father's death. I do not normally go in for such morbid self-probings, but since reading the letters my father had written to Molly I had begun to wonder whether he had something to do with the vehemence of my reactions. A child might well feel strong, if irrational, guilt over such a death, confused and compounded by resentment at his mother's re-marriage, and try to bury these feelings deep as he could. But their ghosts, or something like them, may have been at my shoulder as I stumbled in panic along the track below the Temple. And then, finding Mr Wither's body . . .

Wondering about this possibility I became increasingly uneasy about its mirror-image. Might not a grown man, unconsciously haunted all his life by those ghosts, sit down and *invent* a chain of memories—persuading himself that they were real—to account to himself for such uneasy presences?

Mercifully I had not got far down the spiral of moral hypochondria before I was given the good shaking which was all I needed. A letter arrived out of the blue from Dobbs which put all that out of my mind by giving me something concrete and exciting to think about. And to do.

Dear Rogers,

A breakthrough has occurred, I suspect much better news for me than it may be for you. Richard Smith has answered my advertisement, more than a month after its last appearance. He is willing to see me. The maddening thing is that though I am now said to be on the mend, there is no chance of my getting out of here for at least a couple of months; and as the man is over eighty, surely, I cannot well ask him to journey down here. Yet I feel in my bones it is vital to make contact with him at once. I simply must know how he is going to affect my book; and it would be too sickening if he should die before I am up and about, though he writes in a firm enough hand—very small and neat, much as you describe it.

May I ask you, as a great favour to me, if you will go and see him? I will compile a list of questions I need to have answered, but they are secondary; really I want you to spy out the land. If in your opinion he is hale enough to last till I emerge, I would much prefer to conduct detailed interviews myself; but before that, if at all possible, I need to know what shape and weight the section dealing with him is likely to need. It is (I can trust you to understand this) as much a matter of architecture as of getting the facts right.

Will you take this on? I leave it to you how to approach Smith. I feel this to be a good omen; we shall dish the woman yet. You know, that is something more than a manner of speaking. Somehow she killed her lovers, sucking the life from them to feed her own ebullience. She has been killing me, and my book. But now my doctor begins to say good things, and Richard Smith is alive.

Sorry to exult so, when this may well queer your pitch. Still, it might have been worse for you if you had gone ahead and published, with RS alive and fully recognisable. He lives at 98 Mortimer Court, London SW3. He does not give a telephone number.

Yours,
SD

My reaction was not what Dobbs, or I myself, would have expected. No doubt Dobbs thought that my portrait of the Captain might be libellous. The possibility didn't bother me—the character in my book was a goody, and if there was anything actionable in the details it was only fiction and could be changed. Much more important, the news had come for me, as for Dobbs, at the right moment; I had now used up all there was to use of my own memories of Paddery. I had already decided that I could afford at this point to make the trip down to Devon and look the place over as it was today. It would have been fatal to do this earlier. One is a crystal-gazer in the tent of time. Faint shadows move in the transparent sphere and the lights must be precisely placed, precisely graded, for one to be able to see them at all. Open the flaps, let in the sunlight, and one is looking at an empty glass ball. But now, having seen and recorded all there was by way of shadows, I could begin to compare my perceptions with the real world. Going down to Paddery would be a minor way of doing this, meeting and talking to the Captain much more.

I wrote to him, explaining that Dobbs had asked me to do so because he was writing a life of Isidore Steen. No doubt he knew of Dobbs's reputation. Unfortunately Dobbs was recovering from an illness and would not be able to see Mr Smith for a while, so he had asked me to do a preliminary interview. I did not mention my own acquaintance with him, nor use the title 'Captain' on the envelope. I wanted to approach him as a stranger.

Next morning a woman telephoned. She said she was Mrs Smith and was speaking on behalf of her husband because his hearing made the telephone difficult. Her husband was willing to see me. We fixed an appointment for an afternoon later that week. She sounded disturbingly ordinary for the mate of a creature so exotic in my memories.

I wrote and told Dobbs what was up and asked for his list of questions. When they had not arrived on the morning of my visit I telephoned his secretary. She told me that Dobbs had had a minor relapse and had been ordered not to attempt any work, but had sent her a message that he would still like me to see Smith and spy out the land. She herself sounded anxious about the interview, as if aware that Dobbs was pinning many of his hopes on it. I drove up to London on a fine, warm November morning.

Mortimer Court is one of those Thirties-ish blocks of flats on the south side of King's Road, near Sloane Square. Smith lived on the top floor. I went up in the lift and along a corridor—dark cream walls with debased art deco mouldings. Remembering Mrs Smith's voice, I began to feel a sense of let-down. I would find an old codger with a dim, downtrodden wife living in a tidy dull flat with Regency wallpaper, Redouté prints, gold-tasselled lampshades, dull green armchairs piped with looped gold braid, all done by the Harrods people fifteen years ago. There would be a smelly little dog.

When I rang the bell the exact wife opened the door, apart from her not looking down-trodden—a small woman, some five years older than me, square heavy body in grey twinset (no pearls) and brown tweed skirt; permed grey hair, not blued at all; a look both nervous and eager. I introduced myself, expecting her to withdraw so that I could enter the flat, but she stood and peered at me, then smiled like a child.

'You *are* Rogue Rogers,' she said. 'I thought you must be, from the photographs on your books.'

'Oh . . . well, yes . . . but nobody's . . .'

'I don't expect you remember me. Anne Penoyre. You used to call me Annette.'

'Good Lord! Of course I remember you well, but I didn't . . .'

'Women change more. You'll find Richard's hardly changed at all. He's looking forward to talking to you. I haven't told him who you are. He doesn't approve of me reading detective stories.'

She let me in now. I felt confused, almost shocked. She was in a sense right about my not remembering her, in that she had not at Paddery made any great impression. The Annette Penoyre of my novel was more my fictional creation than most of the other characters, even those with mere walk-on parts such as Stock and Floyd. And yet here she was, living a life wholly untouched by my imaginings, even to the extent of having read some of my books, a detail I would not dream of building into one of my fictional characters. And she had apparently married the Captain when, in my own mind, though she had not necessarily died, she had somehow ceased to exist except as an embodied grief for poor Christopher Wither.

As she led me along a short corridor I saw that I was wrong about this also. Harrods decorators had not set foot here. The paint was dead white, the carpet black, the inner wall covered with a large and ancient-looking oriental hanging, picturing monsters and demons, the colours as ferocious as the gestures and grimaces. It breathed a powerful, musky personality—not a thing I would choose to live with at close quarters. Mrs Smith walked past it unnoticing and opened a door.

'Mr Rogers is here, darling,' she said.

He was standing at the window, looking out, in the

remembered pose. There was a goodish view east and south over the roofs of buildings and the froth of tree-tops towards the tower blocks and spires of the city, all lit with pale wintry sun. I did not feel he was seeing any of this. He seemed not to have noticed our entrance.

Mrs Smith went over and put her hand on his shoulder to catch his attention, but making the gesture into a light caress.

'Mr Rogers is here,' she enunciated. 'Do you want me to fix your deaf-aid?'

He patted the back of her hand as he turned.

'I seem to be hearing today,' he said.

He looked at me and bowed slightly, actor-fashion.

'Mr Rogers,' he intoned.

He had shaved off his moustache.

Though every sound and movement he had made had been true to memory, I still thought for an instant that I'd got the wrong man, so powerfully did that weird growth persist in my mind. Then I realised that, as Mrs Smith had said, he had changed very little. His eyes were the same, large, deep-sunk, dark brown, very bloodshot round the rims. His head was quite bald and his face more mottled than at Paddery; it was also immensely handsome, a model for a bust in the grand manner, old, imperious, marked but not marred by vicissitudes endured. For some reason I thought of Rimbaud at Harar, refusing to discuss the incredible poems of his youth, merely dismissing them as absurd and disgusting.

'It's very good of you to see me, sir,' I said.

He nodded.

'You sit there,' he said. 'Don't wait for me. I move slowly these days.'

I stood till Mrs Smith had left the room, then sat and watched him cross with careful steps to a cushionless wheel-back armchair. He had shed a lot of flesh, but had also lost that look of weightlessness, that odd appearance of floating, that had been produced by his light, quick, silent gait. The room was a well-lit clutter; a lot of books, both on shelves and in piles; a big desk covered with papers; several pictures

—oddly hung, probably not at random but not according to any design I could see—and in varied styles but all producing a strong, rather uncomfortable effect, whether by strident colour or harsh outlining or the nature of the subject portrayed. I had no idea how good they were, but one was either a Munch or the work of an imitator. The same quality of energetic disquiet emerged from the many objects—masks, old weapons, pots and so on—that littered the room. Nothing dominated, unless it was Smith's own personality. I got the impression of a man who needed his sensations full-flavoured, to say the least. I remembered the amount of mustard old Stock used to put on his food when he ate with the boys—he was the only person I have ever seen smear mustard on rice pudding. In a much more complex way Smith, or so I guessed, needed his messages from beyond the barrier of the senses to come with greater emphasis than most of us could tolerate. Perhaps I had not been so wrong to be reminded of Rimbaud.

When he had settled into his chair he leant forward and stared at me.

'I will not have my wife pestered,' he said.

'I don't think . . .'

'She never knew Isidore. Never set eyes on him.'

'I . . .'

'You will give me an undertaking on this, on behalf of Dobbs.'

'Oh, I think so.'

'Not good enough.'

I hesitated.

'Of course Dobbs is an extremely responsible biographer . . .' I began.

'I have read all his books, I believe. Well?'

Suddenly I thought I saw what he was bothered about. Suppose Dobbs made him into a nine-day wonder, Steen's last lover, still alive, still bearing metaphorically the stigmata of the embraces of genius, then journalists might start ringing the bell—'How exactly does it feel, Mrs Smith . . .' I knew this had happened in the case of one of Lytton Strachey's young men after Holroyd's biography had appeared.

'I will undertake that neither Dobbs nor anyone connected with the book will approach your wife without your express permission,' I said.

'That will have to do.'

It wouldn't keep the journalists at bay, I thought, but it was rather touching. How strange, in view of what I had just decided about Smith preferring his sensations pungent, that he should have so mild and bland a wife, and apparently get on so well with her. I made a mental clearing of my throat, preparatory to explaining my anomalous position, but he spoke again.

'I see there is to be a film of Isidore's life,' he said.

'Yes, there was something in one of the Sundays a couple of weeks ago.'

'The company in question have purchased the film rights to Mr Dobbs's biography.'

'So I gather. Steen's books must be out of copyright.'

'In 1977. I wish to be employed as technical adviser to this film.'

'Oh . . .'

'Those are my terms for co-operating with Mr Dobbs.'

'I'm in no position . . .'

'I am aware of that. Let me tell you, Mr Rogers, that Mr Dobbs cannot complete his book, nor can this film be made, without my help. I know major facts, which I believe no one else has had access to. For two years after the war I knew Isidore better than anybody else. I was his catamite, but I was also his confidant. I see that they have taken it into their heads to hire a major American star to play the part of Mary Benison. Nobody apart from myself knows the truth about Isidore's relationship with her. And he did not only talk with me about the present. To take another example, I am in a position to rebut Baston's thesis about the inaccuracy of *To Live like the Jackal*. That is to say Isidore told me which parts of the story were true, and which fudged.'

'Good lord! Why . . .'

'Because I chose. I may tell you that I saw Mr Dobbs's advertisements for me in *The Times*, and ignored them. Later I changed my mind. What I do is no one's business but my own. Well?'

'May I think for a moment, sir? This is a bit unexpected.'

It seemed natural to call him 'sir'. His authority had remained formidable. I did not find myself mentally reverting to the status of school-child in his presence—in fact I knew myself to have in many ways the advantage of him, being aware for instance that the post he was after in connection with the film was likely neither to be in Dobbs's gift nor as lucrative as Smith evidently imagined—but I certainly realised the need to be careful.

'There is a preliminary difficulty,' I said at last. 'As I told you in my letter, Simon Dobbs has been ill—extremely ill, as a matter of fact—and though he is said to be now on the mend it will be some weeks before he is in a position to come and see you, or even to conduct serious negotiations about what you want. Presumably he would have to mediate between you and the film company. What you're asking for may or may not turn out to be straightforward, but from my own experience I know that film deals are peculiarly troublesome to tie down. You cannot count on anything until you have a signed contract in your hand. So I don't think that even if Dobbs were here in my place he would be in a position to agree to your suggestion. The line I think he would take is this. He would need positive evidence that what you have to offer is worth it. For instance, what you say about *To Live like the Jackal* is interesting, but I happen to know that Dobbs has already come to conclusions which sound fairly like what you would confirm.'

'He is guessing. I know.'

'I'm not saying he wouldn't be glad of confirmation, only that it mightn't be a sufficient inducement to him to do what you want, let alone to persuade the film company that your services are indispensable. But suppose you were able to throw some light on Steen's dramatic shift from optimism to pessimism after he had finished *The Fanatics*, that might be of considerable use to Dobbs. Or, from the point of view of the film people, there is the whole mystery of the nature of Steen's relationship with Mary Benison—was it a full-blown love affair? How far did it go? Why did it end? According to the newspaper cutting I saw, the script-writers are still very much in the dark about all that. Do you follow me?'

'I know the answers. That is why I replied to Mr Dobbs's advertisement.'

'Yes, but I'm afraid it's no use your just telling me that, or even telling Dobbs. You won't get anywhere with the film people unless you produce specific facts to prove your value. They watch their budgets these days, however many noughts there are on the final figure. You don't see hangers-on around the sets, the way you did in the Sixties.'

Smith gazed at me without moving. He really had changed extraordinarily little; it was with precisely the same look that he had stared down at me from the staircase when I had come panting in with the news of finding Mr Wither's body. It slightly unnerved me, making me feel that he knew a great deal more about me and my motives than he possibly could.

'Very well,' he said. 'I will answer your second point, but before I do so I must have your signature to a document acknowledging that what I am about to tell you is my copyright. As soon as you are gone I will write out an account of the episode and take steps to formalise my rights in it. If the film is made or the book written making use of this scene without my permission I shall sue. Moreover, I shall if possible make you, Mr Rogers, a party to the action.'

I shrugged inwardly. I didn't think an action against me would stick provided I made the position clear to Dobbs. And anyway, what the hell? I wanted to know.

'All right,' I said, and wrote a couple of lines on my notepad, signed and passed him the sheet. He held it at a distance to read but did not need spectacles.

'Vile writing,' he said. 'That will do. Now, listen with care as I do not propose to repeat myself. I understand that you know something of Mary Benison, but you probably will not have heard of a woman called Désirée O'Connell.'

'She lived with Mary Benison, was remarkably ugly, and wrote French prose-poems signed D.D.'

This was clearly no moment to let on that I knew anything about Molly and her entourage at first hand, but it seemed a good chance to imply that I myself had some status in the world of Steen-research. Smith gave no sign of being impressed.

'Very well,' he said. 'Isidore Steen, as you no doubt know, was for most of his life obsessed with life itself. He felt himself to be an expression of the energies of life, of what Shaw in his crude way used to call the Life Force. The *élan vital* was very current in Isidore's youth, but in his case it was much more than a fashionable notion. It was a genuine expression of his inward being. He believed that life expressed itself in all human activity, but reached its twin peaks, mental and physical, in two processes which he held to be more than merely analogous, to wit artistic creation and sexual creation. Fools wrote him down as an indiscriminate woman-iser, who did not care whom he bedded provided it happened often enough. This is entirely mistaken. I saw him reject apparently attractive women who had made it clear that they were accessible to his attentions. He was also capable of long periods of abstinence. He was never, I think, in love with any woman in the banal sense, but was perfectly prepared to pretend to passion if he thought it would help. He enjoyed play-acting, and did not like success to be too easy. Once an affair was under way he would be very demanding and do his best to get the woman pregnant. He told me that a girl had once come to him to ask him to pay for an abortion and instead he had paid her to have the baby, though she had asked a considerable sum and he had had to borrow. The relationship you would call love was reserved for young men like myself. I do not wish to give the impression that it

156

involved a high degree of passion, but he was a considerate and agreeable lover. You follow me thus far?'

'I think Dobbs is taking much that line.'

'He is a competent biographer. An appreciation of Isidore's approach to women is crucial to understanding what happened between him and Mary Benison. Désirée O'Connell introduced them in 1919. The women had been doing some kind of phoney war-work together. O'Connell was a difficult woman, impossible to like. She drank and she was promiscuous, with a penchant for maimed soldiers, of whom there were a fair number on the Left Bank in those days. She was, as you have heard, so ill-favoured as to be an offence to the eye. She wrote well enough. I myself thought her work interesting and original, though it mined a perverse and narrow seam. Isidore acknowledged that she had talent, but detested both her and her work, to such an extent that I came to believe that there might be an element of fear in his dislike. He celebrated life and she celebrated death, and though he was an infinitely greater artist than she was yet in the end life yields to death. I am trying to present the matter as it might have appeared to Isidore, who saw the world in symbolic terms of that large and simple nature. I cannot tell you categorically that this was how he felt about O'Connell, as he refused to discuss her with me. I used to tease him, pretending to be fascinated by her ugliness. His revulsion was if anything aggravated by her becoming passionately in love with him.

'Of course, you will say, he could have avoided her. That was not, in his eyes, the case, because on meeting Mary Benison he had immediately decided to make her the object of his pursuit. At first the matter appeared straightforward, as the woman was beautiful, far from prudish, and emanated an exultation in life which Isidore felt matched his own. She seemed to respond, and both Isidore and I assumed it would be only a matter of days before he got her to bed, but this turned out not to be the case. She was prepared to go in for any amount of what is now called fore-play, but she would not let him screw her. At first I was amused. I egged Isidore on. I thought it did him good to be shown the door occasionally. Then as the weeks and months went by I began to be bored with the affair. He talked and thought about it a great deal too much. It became an obsession. I have sometimes wondered since whether Isidore may not have been subconsciously aware that a major illness was about to afflict him. Certainly he often spoke as though Mary Benison represented, in some sense, a last chance. I have implied that he was incapable of passionate personal love, but his pursuit of Benison became in the end a passion. That it was love, I doubt.

'For myself, after a while I took a dislike to Benison because of the effect she was having on Isidore and his work. With very few exceptions I have found the human species a despicable lot. Isidore was one of those exceptions and I, being then nineteen, did not like to see him behaving as though that were not the case.

'The pursuit lasted over two years. I have an excellent memory and will describe, provided Mr Dobbs makes suitable arrangements, a number of incidents worth recording, not merely as examples of the humiliation of genius. It was during this period that Isidore was writing *The Fanatics*, and I typed it out for him, page by page, as it came from his pad. I was aware almost from the beginning that it was a dead birth, the failure of a novel potentially comparable with *Crime and Punishment*. After a while I came to believe, as I do to this day, that Benison was somehow responsible for this failure. The woman had it in her to undo and destroy the creative process. *En ton désastre ira ma destinée; Pour abuser les poëtes je suis née.* She and O'Connell were two sides of a coin. It is necessary to understand this if you are to appreciate how the affair ended.

'Throughout 1921 Isidore and I shared an apartment in the old Palais Royal, and Benison and O'Connell a studio in the rue de l'Université. *The Fanatics* was published in the spring of 1922 and the women held a party to celebrate. You will remember that Joyce's *Ulysses* had just appeared, published by an American woman, Sylvia Beach, who ran a small bookshop, because nobody else would risk it. Benison had taken it into her head that she wanted to do the same for *The Fanatics* and Isidore had almost consented to this, despite his London and New York publishers being perfectly prepared to take the book. I persuaded him otherwise, though with some difficulty. In the end it had meant my taking the manuscript over to London myself, to make certain Benison did not contrive to wheedle it off him. In consequence Benison appeared to go out of her way to see that I did not enjoy the party, and I left early. Before I left a good deal had been drunk, and O'Connell, as was her habit, had become obstreperous and then violent. Benison dealt with her ruthlessly, giving her a tumbler of brandy which caused her to pass out in the kitchen.

'Benison herself had been in extremely high spirits and paying a lot of attention to Isidore, not in the sense of making up to him, but constantly pushing in to any conversation he might be having. He regarded talk as a serious activity, essential for the refining of ideas—that was why he refused to live in London. Benison would interrupt, break the flow, send his interlocutor on some errand, and then dash away herself. It is, of course, always impossible to tell with such a person how calculated any pattern of action may be. I assumed that she was teasing Isidore for not having let her publish the book. I was, at any rate, happy to leave.

'I was asleep when Isidore came into the bedroom and sat down on the bed. There was a perfectly good bed in the other room which he would normally have used on such an occasion; indeed I had seen that it was ready for him.

'"Finished," he said.

'I swore at him and turned over, but he dragged me up with a violence he had never used on me before. For a small man he was remarkably strong. As soon as I was well awake I saw that he was agitated. He at once began to tell me what had happened after I had left the party.

'First, Benison had extended her conversation-disrupting activities by making everybody play children's games. This was a habit of hers, but not one likely to be appreciated in French literary circles. Guests began to leave, but when Isidore made a move she asked him to stay to help put O'Connell to bed. She said she also wanted to talk to him. She then literally turned everybody else out, and in half an hour they had the studio to themselves. They picked O'Connell up and carried her into the bedroom. Mary gathered some cushions into a pile, sat down and told Isidore to sit beside her. She asked him what he proposed to write next. He thought that she was trying to persuade him to produce something that she could publish, and started to tell her about a short satiric animal fable he had in mind, which might have been suitable. He had already discussed it with me. Almost at once Mary broke off and went and fetched two huge glasses of brandy.

'Isidore was not a great drinker. I have seen him become boisterous on his share of one bottle of Vosne Romanée. He tried to refuse, but Benison told him that she was going to need it and asked him to help her. At this point he guessed what might be coming, though he had in the past tried the effect of getting her drunk, without success. There is a strong psychological element here; I have mentioned Isidore's belief in a link between artistic creation and sexual activity; he felt he had had an exhausting struggle in writing *The Fanatics*, and the same could be said of his pursuit of Benison. Moreover, there was an explicit relation between the two, as the opening sequence of the novel is based on Benison's own account of her childhood, and he thought it was this that had released him to write the whole book. In his eyes, she was the muse of *The Fanatics*. I, as you know, think the contrary, but for him the writing and the pursuit were interwoven activities. He had brought off the former, and now he was going to achieve the latter. Benison of course knew of her role in the book. He had done her his utmost honour in so immortalising her, and now she was going to reward him. She needed the brandy to overcome her inhibitions.

'These are my own speculations. Isidore told me merely the order of events as they had occurred.

'They talked a little about the fable. They drank. They kissed. They fondled. They undressed each other. When they were both naked Benison stood and pulled him to his feet and turned him round. She had been wearing black silk stockings and with these she bandaged his eyes. He was aware of being rather drunk, but convinced that his hour had come.

'"Blind man's buff," she said. "When you catch me you can have me."

'He noticed that she said "when", not "if".

'He groped around the studio. She did not run away and hide but circled close, darting in to touch him here and there and giggling all the while. At first she was wary, but then she seemed to become bolder, lingering closer, stimulating him, touching his genitals . . .

'And then he had her by the elbow. She barely struggled before she flung her arms round him and pulled him down on to the cushions. He was on her, in her, astonished by her greed for him . . .

'You will of course have guessed what had happened. It was the other woman who, for once, had been merely feigning drunk. The whole thing had been planned. Even while O'Connell had been dancing closer and closer to Isidore, stimulating him, then letting him catch her, Benison had been behind her shoulder, gasping and laughing. And now at the climax of his imagined triumph he felt hands at the knot of his blindfold, saw the face of O'Connell contorted beneath him, heard Benison's voice in his ear, saying "Boo!"

'He disengaged himself and staggered to his feet. She ran to the bedroom, turned in the doorway, kissed her finger to him, went in and locked the door.'

'Good lord,' I said.

'A ridiculous incident.'

'But . . .'

'Is that all? Is that Isidore Steen's heart of darkness? I laughed when he told me, delighted that the affair was now irrevocably over. He stared at me for a while. I apologised. He rose and left the room. I heard him moving around but was asleep by the time the outer door opened and closed. When I got up I found on my typewriter an envelope full of money and a note saying that I could stay in the apartment as long as it lasted. I chose not to. I used the money to buy a passage to Rangoon. I did not meet or correspond with Isidore Steen again.'

I felt dazed. My mind was full of an image of Molly stalking up on me behind the Spanish chestnut, and how my heart bounded when she said 'Boo!' in my ear.

'The incident, though true, has symbolic weight,' said Smith. 'And I think you will agree that it also has what they call box-office potential.'

'What did he do?'

'What could he? I believe that he already knew in his heart that *The Fanatics* was still-born, and I suspect that the incident—his pursuit of Benison being so bound up in his writing of the book—may have brought that knowledge into the open. When the one ended in an appalling and humiliating *débâcle*, he found the same was true of the other. All he could do was take his revenge in his own way, though few would have recognised it as such. Very effective it turned out to be.'

I was hardly listening. Another confirmatory parallel had struck me.

'She cheated over the brandy, of course,' I said.

'What are you talking about?'

'The tumbler she gave Daisy. It would have been tea or something. And the same when she sat down to drink with Steen—hers wouldn't have been brandy. Don't you remember, with the naval officers at Paddery . . .'

I looked up to see his gaze on me, all its old ferocious power, its sense of somehow abstract malevolence, glaring out from the red-rimmed eyes. He had told his story in a level, deep, near-whisper. Not even his account of the climax, or his mention of its erotic potential in the cinema, had altered his tone. I had wondered whether the story was rehearsed—he had implied that he had not told it before, and perhaps the ordered and formal syntax was natural to him. In a sense I had been a lay figure, a mere intermediary through whom he was speaking to Dobbs. Now, for the first time, he turned the full energy of his personality—undiminished by age—on me.

'We've met before,' I explained. 'I didn't mention it because I didn't want to confuse the issue, but I'm glad it's come up. I've always wanted a chance to thank you. You were about the best teacher I ever had.'

I thought he hadn't heard me. He continued to stare at me with what seemed a mixture of hatred and distrust.

'A contemptible profession,' he said suddenly. 'Now I am tired and must ask you to go. It seems to me that I have told you more than enough to persuade Mr Dobbs that my assistance is absolutely necessary to him. You will make it clear that I retain the copyright in this matter. I expect an immediate answer.'

'I'll write to him as soon as I get home,' I said. 'His secretary tells me he's had a bit of a relapse, but assuming he gets over it he should be able to make a preliminary response in a week or so. If there's going to be any serious delay I'll let you know.'

He closed his eyes.

'That will have to do,' he said.

I left.

Mrs Smith was waiting for me in the passage. I wanted to speak to her anyway, to get the telephone number, but she put her finger to her lips and beckoned. I followed her further up the passage into another sitting-room, smaller than her husband's and furnished with run-of-the-mill chintzes. The only untidiness came from a sewing-basket on the floor. She seemed to have been working on a petit-point stool-cover, to a design supplied by a shop.

'I do hope you don't mind,' she said in a low voice. 'I can't resist asking you to sign one of your books for me.'

'Of course not. I'll do as many as you've got.'

'Oh, how kind of you. I didn't dare ask.'

She had half a dozen, hardback, with a nice, thoroughly-read look. I sat down, found a pen and started to put my name on the fly-leaves.

'Did you tell him who you were?' she asked.

'Only by accident.'

'Oh . . . what did he say?'

'Not much. He didn't seem too pleased.'

'You mustn't mind that. He's got such terribly high standards about books and things. That's why I sneaked you in here like this. I don't want him teasing me about the sort of nonsense I like reading. Oh dear, I shouldn't have said that.'

'I won't take it to heart.'

One learns there's no point in being upset—the valuation is probably just—but one can't help it. Mrs Smith was such a thoroughly nice woman that I minded less than sometimes. One cannot expect people who don't belong to the book world to pick their phrases with delicacy. She must have been thinking along the same lines.

'You wouldn't think, would you, that I had literary blood in my veins?' she said.

'It's not hereditary. My family were lawyers and politicians mostly.'

She took the books from me and put them back on the shelf. They clearly had their own places in what was a useful collection from the narrow field in which I work, the genre of pure detective story, lying somewhere between the crime novel and the thriller. I was about to ask if she'd like me to get Harry Keating's signature when she said, turning the last book over in her hands, 'I hope you make a reasonable living out of it, Mr Rogers.'

'Provided I keep writing.'

'At least you're still in copyright.'

'Not much use when you're out of print.'

'Oh, I suppose not.'

As she led me to the front door she took no special trouble to creep past her husband's room, or perhaps she relied on his deafness. It struck me as odd that that impressive intelligence could be so simply misled—how little any of us know about each other. And even when we attempt to communicate, how easily the signals are garbled, as with Mrs Smith's response to my telling her how her husband had reacted on finding out who I was. That one word 'who' had meant two different people, in his case a child, in hers a writer. Strange.

As she held the front door she looked up into my eyes and said, 'You will do your best for us, won't you? For old times' sake . . . Rogue.'

'I'll try, but it's not really in my hands. I'm just a messenger.'

'We've had a marvellous life. It would be so sad to spoil it now. He's older than he looks.'

'I'll do my best. I owe him something.'

'Oh, so do I!'

'Well, goodbye.'

'Goodbye. Thank you for coming. I'm glad it was you.'

13

I barely noticed the journey home to Hampshire. My autonomous driving system took over while my conscious mind tried to sort itself out. Even there I seemed to have several levels of preoccupation. At the surface my first concern was to make sure I had the story clear for Dobbs. I had taken a tape-recorder along to the interview but confronted by Smith's vehemence over copyright had not even suggested using it. This didn't worry me—though I could not have repeated what he said word for word I had all its details vivid in my mind. I ran these inward spools a couple of times to prove to myself that this was so.

Then, still at the surface level, I started to wonder whether the story was true. It smelt of contrivance, but whose? Molly's, or Smith's? I felt that Dobbs, lacking my memories of Paddery, was likely to plump for Smith. Even on psychological grounds, insofar as the mind of such a man is readable, it seemed a Smith-like contrivance; *Measure for Measure* was his kind of play. It was clear he needed the money; he had every incentive to make his contribution seem indispensable, to invent scenes which would appeal to the box-office . . . I swore at myself for not asking Mrs Smith whether he went much to the cinema—it would have been a help to know whether he realised that Miss Remick was unlikely to consent to play the scene he had described to me . . .

But he had told me something very close to the truth. I was sure of that. Or rather I was sure that Molly had at some point played blind man's buff with a would-be lover, substituted Daisy for herself and then said 'Boo!' in the man's ear. There was the detail about the fake drinks, too. And Steen's revulsion from Daisy. It was strange to me, because nothing Smith had said about Steen had mitigated my dislike of the man, that I so deeply understood how he had felt over this. I realised I had not cared for Daisy at all. She had frightened me badly, though in between the first meeting in the chestnut grove and my nightmare on the track to the Temple I had managed to tell myself that my fear was only that she would do or say something to embarrass me. And . . .

Yes, there was something else to do with Daisy, some other parallel. I was aware of its presence at a deeper level, as one is aware of a large fish in dark water, not by seeing the animal but by vague stirrings in its element. Anyway, I had no doubt I was going to tell Dobbs that as far as I was concerned Smith's story was ninety per cent true, at least. After all, hadn't I promised little Mrs Smith I would do my best for them?

The conscious thought of her made me realise that all the time since we met on her doormat I had been in a state of mild shock at the strangeness of her marriage. The short interview in her sitting-room had if anything added to the feeling. She said they'd had a marvellous life. She talked as though she had nothing whatever to hide, apart from her taste in books. She assumed I knew all about her. Perhaps it was because of this openness, this lack of mystery and secrets, that I was well down the M3 before I realised that she must be Daisy's daughter. And, if Smith's story were true, by Isidore Steen.

The reader probably got there pages ago—the experienced reader three chapters ago. In fact the experienced reader will know by now how Christopher Wither died, and at whose hand (the latter question pretty obvious, I'd have thought). This is just an example of the artificiality of the genre, of all fiction perhaps, in that it takes place outside you, allows you to inspect it, choose your distance from it and so on; whereas with real happenings you take place inside them, and the more closely they concern you the less likely you are to be able to grasp the relationship of their individual parts. In detective fiction, with the demand that the plot should function as a mechanism, the relationship of those parts has to be unreally precise and clear, and the reader has to remain well outside. Since this story seems to have got into book form after all, I feel it is only polite to apologise to the reader for not presenting him with his customary obfuscations. Where was I? Half-way down the M3.

I pulled over into the slow lane and drove the next stretch at forty. I began to see things, to feel some of that excitement that is generated when the plot of a new book starts pulling itself together and one's random and disparate inventions turn out to slot into each other as if they had been designed to do so. At first the excitement was attended by the same kind of pleasure, but gradually, as I could not resist picking away at the scab that had grown over those old wounds, pleasure gave way to alarm, and then to horror.

Steen had died in 1927. The date had stuck in my mind because of the mild coincidence of it being the year I was born. The copyrights, as Smith had said, had expired in 1977. Mrs Smith had also talked wistfully about living on copyrights. That was what they had been doing. That was why Smith had married her—for the copyrights of *To Live like the Jackal* and *The Fanatics*. I got a *frisson*, perhaps my first intimation that I was dealing with something other than an intellectual game, from the title of Steen's big money-spinner. In the book it had been von Lettow-Vorbek who was the lion and Steen himself the attendant scavenger; but now I saw that I could cast Steen as the great predator, his books as his prey, and those who subsequently lived squabbling on their proceeds as the jackals. Yes, wasn't there something in one of Dobbs's letters to me about money no longer coming in from the trust after the war. That must have been because Smith had by then married Annette, and taken over the income from royalties. And . . .

I had something for Dobbs! I knew why Steen had set up that peculiar trust, with its uncharacteristic secretiveness! What had Smith said? 'All he could do was take his revenge in his own way, though few would have recognised it as such.

Very effective it turned out to be.' The trust was no act of generosity, let alone of forgiveness. It was a way of binding Molly and Daisy to each other in mutual parasitism. I shivered at the thought, much as I had some forty years ago as the frost fingered in through the smashed panes of Lord Orne's conservatory. How extraordinary it was to think that I had gone back there the very next Sunday and found a tarpaulin over the holes, and that by the end of that term Molly had caused the glass to be found (curved panes, in wartime!) and we were all behaving as though it had never happened.

Or was it so extraordinary? I mean, did it really happen like that by accident? Isn't it more likely that there was, effectively, a kind of conspiracy with Molly at its centre, whereby all concerned deliberately behaved as though that evening had never occurred? At least nothing was done to prevent me continuing to go down to Molly's teas until the end of next summer term, when I left. I don't think Daisy went 'mad' again. I don't even remember feeling apprehensive that she might.

Nor, of course, do I remember the slightest indication that Annette and the Captain might end up married. He continued to tutor me, she to teach Freshers, which meant I saw very little of her up at the school, and I don't think he came down to the conservatory again, so I would seldom have seen them together . . .

My mind gave up the effort at recollection and slithered to a different sort of strangeness, if you can call Mrs Smith's straightforward pleasant ordinariness by that name. Was it thinkable that she had been begotten under the circumstances Smith had described to me? Ought not such parents, such a conjunction, to have produced, if not a monster, at least some hint of the bizarre? Of course Daisy was promiscuous, Smith had said. Steen didn't need to be the father, only to believe he was. Or perhaps not even that. For the sake of his revenge his fatherhood could be considered a handy fiction. Perhaps Mrs Smith's real father was one of those maimed soldiers, able in spite of his deformities to pass on good sound genes.

Up through this speculation, released perhaps by my stirring around in the pool of memory a few minutes before as I thought of the broken panes in the conservatory, floated the thought I had been trying to embody half an hour ago, the other parallel that verified Smith's story. It was between Daisy becoming violent in the studio in the rue de l'Université and her doing the same that night at Paddery. As I stared at the two mental images side by side I saw that the resemblance went deeper than the surface. They both had been put-up jobs. They both, even, had involved Molly pouring out drinks which were not what they appeared. Molly had arranged for Daisy to go mad, that particular night and none other.

I was actually turning into my driveway when a whole new set of possibilities struck me. Not new facts, but re-arrangements of the mixture of facts and what I had taken to be fictions, which I had thought of as my novel. In this new alignment the whole bang shoot was true. Not 'true'. True.

I had a cup of tea and then settled down and wrote to Dobbs. I hadn't been keeping carbons of my letters to him, but this time, in case he wanted to refer to some detail, I did. The account of my interview with Smith, as printed in the previous chapter, is taken from this carbon, with only two or three later interpolations about my own reactions. For completeness, and because of a couple of things she said, I included my talk with Mrs Smith. I had supper at my desk. It was twenty past twelve when I finished, well after my normal bedtime, but there was no question of being able to go away and sleep.

All the time I had been writing—stimulated, indeed, by the familiar process—my idea about the death of Christopher Wither had continued to grow, to make connections, to become a complex life threshing around like a child in the womb. To quiet it I needed not only to get it down on paper but to communicate it to someone. There was no other possible audience than poor Dobbs. I would have to write him a second letter. But though I had the excuse that a small part of the structure—that concerned with the trust set up for Annette—was relevant to a life of Steen, it did not seem fair to lumber a sick man with another great dollop of reading when what I had already written for him was difficult enough to cope with. All the same I had to get the stuff not merely written but posted, so I resolved on what may seem a childish stratagem. Our post is collected at 9.15 a.m.; I would catch that with my first letter, putting a first-class stamp on it; then, as soon as the van was gone I would post my second letter, second-class. Thus I would get them off my chest almost simultaneously and Dobbs would receive them at least a couple of days apart.

Dear Dobbs,

I'm extremely sorry to burden you with a second great screed. Really I'm only writing it in order to get to sleep, and very likely shan't send it. If I do, please feel free to treat it as the next batch of 'light hospital reading'. There won't be any more of the novel. That's over, done with, impossible. But if you want you can regard this as the final instalment, where the detective unravels the apparent tangle that has gone before. Except that he doesn't . . .

No, I'm sorry, that won't do. The thing is, I'm out of my depth, emotionally as well as intellectually. I don't know how to cope, and feel the only hope is to consult somebody who is used to evaluating historical events. Since you already know most of the facts (if facts they are), you're the obvious person. So, though in one sense I'm perfectly happy for you to read this as a sort of botched sketch of a conclusion to my novel, in another sense I'd be grateful if you could think about it seriously.

Look, suppose you'd been writing a life of Molly Benison, and suppose the events in my novel and what I'm now going to add to them had come to you in the form of the reminiscences of some witness of doubtful veracity, how would you evaluate them?

I ought to be able to do the job myself, but I can't. I'm too confused, too involved, too shaken, I suppose. It seems absurd to suggest that shock can be delayed forty years, but that's how I feel. It's why I can't do the job myself. I wouldn't bother you if I could think of anybody else.

The intellectual difficulty is obvious. Practically all the evidence I have comes from the chapters of my novel. It didn't exist as a conscious memory until I wrote it down. What's more, a number of vital points are of even shakier stature—I actually put them in as clues to my fictional plot. There are quite straightforward literary reasons for me to have invented them. (There are also, let me admit it, other and less straightforward reasons for my having invented the whole rigmarole, a set of psychological loadings which nudged my imagination in that direction. I won't go into these now. They can also be deduced from the novel. I confess they are there, probably.)

All I can answer is this: I have long believed that one registers all one's experience, but only notices about five per cent of it. The rest is there, stored in usually inaccessible memory banks. But fragments emerge unpredictably to prove that the banks exist. Every smell I have known, every face I have seen, every dream I have dreamed is in them. Writing my novel made me feel—as I've several times tried to explain to you—as though I had chanced on the code which gave me access to that bit of the banks.

But it's not just sensations which are in them. There are ideas too, glimpses of knowledge, connections made forty years ago between fact and fact. I was quite a clever child, you know. Not brilliant, but quick. In a sense, that was my peak period. I don't think, for all its acquired experience, my brain has ever functioned as efficiently as it did then. It seems to me quite possible that I not merely perceived things, but began to make connections between them. I began to realise that Molly had been involved in something unspeakable, but never let the knowledge surface because I wanted to be able to go on adoring her. But the knowledge remained, half-formed, uncompleted business waiting its time. Then, when the chance came, when I was not only thinking about Paddery, but looking for individual details to knot into a network around a crime, it presented me with these long-hoarded, long-frustrated frets.

Do you follow me? Do you believe me? Do *I* believe me? Emotionally yes, intellectually no. Intellectually I have to accept that Christopher Wither was nearly certainly killed by a rogue stag (which was what the inquest decided), and that my attempt to think otherwise is self-delusion, an effort to glorify one of my fancy worlds with the status of fact, a long dissatisfaction with the worthwhileness of what I write final-ly released into action by my correspondence with you.

But at the emotional level I cannot get away from the conviction that there is something there, something that caused the emotion in the first place, caused my extreme involvement with this particular book, caused me to let it get so badly out of hand, caused me to find it impossible to write apparently promising sections and then to feel a great sense of release as I coped with other bits which weren't really part of my plan at all—my original plan, that is—but which then turned out to have more and more relevance as the plot of my novel changed to bring it steadily closer to what I now think—now feel, I mean—was the truth.

One point which you may not appreciate—I don't im-agine you find time to read much of my sort of book. The 'solution' I am going to give you would, if it occurred in a modern detective novel, seem ludicrously old-fashioned. I'm not much of a hand at plots, but I think my fingers would recoil from the keys rather than type out in a MS some of what you're going to read. It is genuinely not something I would choose to invent as an author anxious for his reputation. Why, then, each time I picked up some fresh detail and saw how it slotted into place, did something in me give it a very powerful 'Yes'? But it did. And said 'No' to aesthetically much more satisfying notions. These yeses and noes are things I am now compelled to account for just as much as if they were so many bloody thumb-prints. When I adduce details of my novel as evidence for my theory, will you accept that however fictional it may seem each of these details had such a 'Yes' behind it? That's the most I can ask.

My very first point is doubly internal—something inside me when I wrote my last instalment nine days ago, and something else inside me forty years back. If you look at that episode you will see that when Paul reaches the Temple he is overcome by a wave of terror whose central element is that the business of Daisy's 'going mad' had been *arranged* to get him there. I do remember thinking this. Truly. And I now think that both the idea and the terror represent one of those childhood perceptions of a truth, half understood and then promptly buried, about which I wrote just now. It is perfectly clear to me, and I'm sure was to you when you read it, that the passage in my book about Daisy 'going mad' in fact describes her reaching her fighting-drunk stage; and it's almost as clear that Molly was waiting for this to happen. But neither of these now obvious points were present in my mind when I wrote those pages. They didn't occur to me till I was driving home from seeing Smith and was struck by the way what he had told me about Daisy's seduction of Steen in the studio echoed the incident in the conservatory. Reflected, rather than echoed. Mirror-images. In the studio, Daisy was sober when she was assumed drunk; in the conservatory 'mad' (i.e. drunk) when she was assumed sane (sober); in both places with Molly's connivance, with deception over the drinks, and with a hideous deed as the end-product.

Have you any doubt that in the conservatory episode Daisy was drunk? Didn't you tell me that Apollinaire or someone had seen her at a party drunk and throwing things 'as usual'. Now Smith has confirmed this trait. But she reached this stage that afternoon when all she'd had to drink for some while was, apparently, tea. Molly was pouring the cups out at the drinks table, by the teapot. Molly had organised things so that the tea-drinking went on longer than usual. The only explanation I can see for Daisy's behaviour is that Molly got her drunk, deliberately, by lacing her tea with gin.

Why? For fun, do you think? To watch her beat up the sailors? But she needed the sailors to keep her in gin. The only outcome I know of is that Annette was prevented from keeping her appointment with Wither, or rather, delayed in doing so for about an hour.

I'd better deal with Annette. Here, at least, are some facts from outside the novel. She married Smith. His first serious remark to me expressed strong anxiety that she should not be 'pestered', and was accompanied by the assertion that she had never seen Steen. Who, in that case, would want to pester her? Anyway, they have been reasonably well off—the rent of those flats must always have been highish—but are now short of money. There is a strong suggestion that they have been living on copyrights which expired a little while ago. Smith actually mentioned 1977 as the date of expiry of the Steen copyrights. Molly was getting an income from that source before the war but not after it, and even while she was getting it she was hoarding like a manic squirrel. Smith used an odd phrase to me in describing what Steen did after the studio episode: 'All he could do was take his revenge in his own way, though few would have recognised it as such. Very effective it turned out to be.' After his break with Steen Smith left at once for the Far East, didn't he, and only re-surfaced —as far as we know—in 1940. Will you accept the implication that the last few words probably refer to what he discovered when he arrived at Paddery, to wit that Molly and Daisy were still living together, Daisy in a permanent mild stupor?

There is one reference inside the novel to a likeness between Annette and Daisy, not in appearance but in the use of a gesture. When I put this in it carried no plot weight—it was just a remembered event. But I'm now pretty well certain that Annette was Daisy's daughter, probably by

175

Steen, or if not then represented to him as being so. I think Steen devised his trust with its strange set-up with the deliberate aim of binding Molly and Daisy together in a state of mutual parasitism. The money theoretically went to Daisy, for the child, and would then go to Annette herself when she was twenty-one. Steen can't, of course, have foreseen precisely how the relationship would evolve, but you told me he believed strongly in the corruptingness of money; he set up a trust in which the effect would have maximum chance to operate. (I would guess that Molly took Daisy at her most awful along to meet the trustees; in my experience such men would be only too grateful to have the mess of dealing with such a person removed from them—Molly would have been able to charm them blind, anyway.) Presumably there would have been some kind of accounting when Annette was twenty-one, but Molly would have been able to hang on to most of what she'd salted away, claiming it as rent and living expenses for the three of them over the years.

Do you know, for all the physical horror of the events in the studio and the Temple, this now seems to me the most appalling—I mean Molly's treatment of Daisy. It's like a female version of Ugolino and the Archbishop in the ninth circle—not just that Molly was prepared to enslave Daisy by keeping her in a gin-haze ('Not too little, not too much, but just right'—remember that?) but herself enduring for the sake of a little money the moral squalor of living with such a person in such circumstances. I wonder what they did when they were alone? Do you happen to know what became of Daisy after 1941? She was still around when I left Paddery for the last time in July that year. I used to write to Molly from Eton, but she hardly ever answered and I gave up. Then she was mostly in Paris, wasn't she, after the war, still in and out of the gossip columns, I remember. Did Daisy stay with her, or did Molly put her into a home? Or let her drink herself to death? Or did she actually *need* Daisy, for her own mysterious reasons? Which would be worse? Ugh. Anyway, that's why she had to keep conjuring gin out of the navy.

I'm supposed to be writing about Annette. She doesn't, I'm aware, make a strong impression in the novel, presumably because she didn't on me. I was intending to work her up in the second draft, give her a bit more solidity. But all I really have is an idea of a clumsy, plain girl, reserved and nervy. There is one short passage in which I suggest a yearning to get away, a point which 'came' as I was writing, in a manner which makes me think it was a genuine impression; a sense of difficulty in her dealings with Molly, a sort of distrust, perhaps; I am able to form no picture at all of how she coped with Daisy. In a fictional world I would need to get this into the open somehow, but I can't. Possibly my failure indicates another area of childhood half-awareness, still buried—something to do with my own closeness to my mother until her re-marriage? So it's not much use saying *that* sort of girl wouldn't throw herself into the arms of an elderly and unlovely suitor, so soon after the nasty death of a lover. I don't know. But suppose she really did long to get away; suppose Wither was at bottom just a chance to do so; suppose also that such a girl, nurtured by sinister matriarchs, should be more than susceptible to the attractions of a father-figure . . . It seems to have worked, that's all I can say.

As for Smith himself, the problem with him is quite different from that with Annette. He made a vivid—violent, almost—impression on me when I was a child, and reconfirmed it yesterday. Externally I know him well—not just his appearance, but the sense of his presence. Still, I have no confidence in guessing what he might, in a given circumstance, actually do. Take the remark which put you on to him—the one about being wanted by the police of five countries—and suppose it's true. This implies that he had no scruples about committing crimes, and also that he had by no means always got away with it. It is a gambler's remark. Not a gambler at calculated odds, either, but one who after long periods of stillness and apparent patience, suddenly acts, and with unpredictable violence. There is still a feral smell (I don't mean that literally) about him. I felt yesterday that I had gone not into a room, but a lair, where a big predator brooded among old bones. (Is this more hindsight? Am I, having decided he might be such a creature, now creating imaginary intuitions about what I felt at the interview? You'll have to make up your mind. I can't.)

Suppose such a man, driven home by the war, middle-aged, after a life of seedy and unsuccessful adventuring, decides the time has come to settle down. Suppose he goes to Paddery to see whether anything can be made of his knowledge of Molly, and there finds that she has, apparently, a source of income. Suppose he then deduces its nature, as I have. Might he not then decide that he could solve his financial problems by marrying this convenient heiress? He would be in no hurry. He knew Molly wouldn't let the affair with Wither come to anything, and he could then catch Annette on the rebound. And Molly wouldn't be able to veto that marriage because of what Smith knew. Meanwhile he would work to become in Annette's eyes a safe friend, a source of counsel and comfort.

The plan went wrong. I now think I actually saw two stages of this happening, on the day when I cut the football match. You will find a brief passage of talk in which I took Captain Smith to be referring to my father's war experiences; in fact he could just as well have been talking about Annette's father—this would explain his spurt of rage at my mention of Molly's acquaintance with my father, when the image he had in his mind was that of Steen. He then took Annette aside while I was ringing the bell and told her that he had known her father. She was thrilled, because I believe nobody had ever told her anything about her parents. And later that day he must have told her more of the story, including the fact that Daisy was her mother. Now she was appalled. I saw them at this stage on the path towards the gardens, if you remember. Annette's vague yearning to escape from Daisy and Molly suddenly became an urgent need. But Smith had precipitated the crisis far too soon for his own purposes, because at that point Annette had somebody else to turn to, somebody with whom she at least imagined herself to be in love. He even had a motor-car, and extra petrol. And there was also a traditional and well-used technique for minors wishing to escape from parents or guardians with the man they loved. Remember? They went to Gretna Green and got married under Scots law. I've just got hold of a press report on the inquest on Wither, and apparently this was what they were planning to do on the night Wither was killed.

You may remember that according to school rumour Wither had had a row with The Man that afternoon and left for good, in his car. He was a very decent chap, you know. He would have recognised the moral compulsion to rescue Annette as over-riding, but at the same time would not have wanted to let The Man down by simply disappearing with Annette. I think he would have gone and asked for time off. The Man, not unnaturally, refused, but to judge by your account of his relations with his junior staff he could well have done so in a manner sufficiently intolerable to cause Wither to blow up and resign. (By the way, when I wrote this passage about the row I thought it was going to be part of a red herring to do with Wither having reported one of the senior staff for buggery, but I didn't invent it for that purpose.) I don't think that at that stage they had planned to run off that very night, but having precipitated matters Wither decided to carry them through. He arranged to come back and meet Annette at the Temple when she was supposed to be walking me home across the park. It was a more sensible place to meet than it may seem. I may not have made the geography clear, but it was half-way between the path from the conservatory to the school and the drive where he would naturally park his car.

I don't know how Smith knew of the sudden plan, but I believe Annette may simply have told him. If I am right about their relationship at that time, she would.

What does Smith do? Try to dissuade her? Tell Molly?

Give up? I don't think any of these. I believe he had already made up his mind that he was going to marry Annette. She was his bride. It was not just a matter of her becoming his meal ticket for the rest of his life, though it's clear to me from my interview with him that this was what in fact happened: for forty years, thanks to her income, he has been able to live in the manner in which he chose. That is quite a powerful motive, but I believe there was a stronger and stranger one. Long ago, barely an hour after Annette had been conceived, he had laughed at her father, and in doing so betrayed the one man of all the human race whom he had ever positively admired. Now he was going to make amends through the daughter, by taking care of her, and seeing that she had a life as satisfactory to herself as he could achieve. (He seems to have brought this off, too. 'Marvellous' she called it.) And now, suddenly, she looked like preventing any of that happening by marrying a particularly naïve and ineffectual member of 'a despicable profession'.

Is this—are these—sufficient motive for murder? For you and me, probably not, but for Captain Smith? We are tame animals—at least I know I am. But with a man like that you can never be sure, any more than a zoo-keeper can of how far he can trust the caged bear he looks after. I don't mean Smith was (is?) a psychopath, just that his compunctions are not ours. I believe things like this had happened before to him, but have no evidence, only the sense of danger I felt as a child. You don't get that from a man who has never done anything to evoke the feeling.

You'll ask, in any case how could he be sure she would have him, with Wither out of the way? But who else was there for her to turn to, what other escape? The bond between them (not, I think, ever a sexual one) was already quite strong. Honestly, that does not seem to me a difficulty, and I do not think it would have to him. The difficulty was to get rid of Wither.

How shall he do it? He has only an afternoon to plan the act. Time and place are chosen for him. It must be around dusk, at the Temple. Shall it be obviously a murder (e.g. shall he use The Man's revolver?) or apparently an accident? Even a gambler would surely choose the accident—a murder would automatically entail a thorough investigation. But what kind of an accident is possible at the Temple? As it happens, there is an obvious one. Old Floyd has been attacked there by a rogue stag. Everybody knows about that.[1]

So can he fake such an accident? Obviously not, if the result is going to be a body mangled with antler-blows and hoof-prints. But the thrust of a single tine through the eye? (This is more likely in any case, if you think about it —animals don't go tramping to and fro over dead victims.) I was already considering this problem when I went to

[1] Footnote, to avoid interrupting the flow, but it's a vital part of the argument. Stags, even in rut, are probably not dangerous. I have read three books on them and talked to a park ranger at Richmond. All four agree that stags can kill, but it's very rare. One of the books refers to a man being killed in a park in Devon about forty years back. The two others say that there is one authenticated instance of an attack pressed home and resulting in a death. It looks as if that instance must have been Wither. Of course we all believed stags were dangerous. It's a widely-held myth—they have boards saying so at all the entrances to Richmond, for instance, though the ranger implied that those were really there to stop the deer being bothered. It was certainly accepted at the inquest on Wither. You might think countrymen would know better, but they didn't. Look what a shambles they made of the cull, for instance. The inquest, incidentally, was held in Exeter. I remember the coroner only vaguely, as a thin grey man in a black suit—a solicitor, I should think, but certainly a townsman. The whole question whether stags do attack people makes much more sense as soon as you accept that Wither was not killed by one, thus removing the only documented instance of such an attack. This, with Smith's marriage to Annette and (if you accept it as true) what he told me yesterday, are facts from the real world, not part of my novel, which have to be accounted for. If it weren't for them I think I could write the whole thing off as my own paranoia.

Richmond—yes, another instance of my now trying to think true what I previously thought I'd invented!—so I looked carefully at antlers. They are not designed for such a task, though spiky enough. They are shaped to make the most of a forward-and-upward curving stroke, slowish, with the mass of the head and neck behind them. But a man needs a spear, a weapon shaped for the sharp thrust of human arms. A spear is a haft and a point. One could of course use a single tine from an antler as a spear-*point*—there's a big one that spikes forward near the root of the antler which would be ideal— and for a haft you would need a stake a few feet long and an inch or more thick.

Smith has seen a boy holding just such a stake. Moreover it has a length of string attached to it, with which the point could be lashed on. As duty master he could have seen where the boy keeps the thing, in a slot between two racks of lockers. And there are loose antlers, picked up by the boys, with the mound of dead deer in the garage. The weapon, therefore, can be made.

Do you think it possible that such a man is influenced by omens? I do. The realisation that the tool he needs is already to hand, provided for him, speaks to the gambler, telling him, 'Yes, now. Your tide is flowing. Take it.' I think it is at this moment that what had been a mere brooding possibility becomes a definite plan, to be thought out and followed through. The timing of the film show is another such omen. Just when Wither will be at the Temple, waiting for Annette (he has told her to come 'as soon as possible'—just a guess—so he himself will be there early) the whole school will be in Big Space watching the film. There weren't many amusements at Paddery. Most of the kitchen staff came, and some of the teachers. Unless there were some unlucky crisis nobody would miss the duty master. Even then he could plausibly have been outside, doing an early check on the black-out.

One problem arises. The drive is tarmac, but the path up to the Temple, though gravelled, has soft patches. He cannot be sure of not leaving a footprint. When Annette gets to the Temple and finds the body, what will she do? Nearly certainly run to the school for help. There is a danger she will then put a footprint on top of one of Smith's, making it clear that he has been there first. The answer is for Smith himself to find the body, or rather to claim to have done so (I'll come to that in a moment). Therefore Annette must not reach the Temple until, say, half an hour after Smith has come off duty. His best hope of that is to get Molly's help to delay her. You remember I found him coming into Long Passage from the entrance hall when I went to ask permission to go out to tea—there was a telephone in the secretary's office, unused on Sundays. I have no idea what he told Molly—it depends whether he had already made approaches to her about his plan to marry Annette. He might have. They'd have understood each other, I think, though I now also think he detested her and she was afraid of him. They could have come to some tacit agreement that he could have Annette provided he didn't enquire where the trust money had been going over the past twelve years. Presumably he wouldn't actually say now that he was going to kill Wither, but he would still be taking a huge risk, because after the act Molly would know that he had done so. Once again, though, she wouldn't be able to say, because then he would have no reason to keep quiet about her peculations. They would each be in a position to betray the other.

(Good lord! A thought! Is it possible that in one of Molly's unopened trunks you will find her account of all this? *This must be why she arranged for you to have them when she died!* I would gladly pay a researcher to sort the papers for you, meanwhile keeping an eye open for such a document. Please consider this.) The possibilities of speculation are endless, but not pointless. Because we come back to the fact that Molly did get Daisy drunk, and the result was to delay Annette. (A point I forgot to make when discussing this earlier: Molly had apparently put off guests who might have helped control Daisy, and the officers were due back at base. No, I don't *remember* either of these details, but they are there in my novel.)

Just as he has finished telephoning, Smith is confronted by the boy who regularly attends Molly's teas. He uses his authority to delay his arrival at the conservatory, on the off-chance that it will also delay his departure, and hence Annette's. This isn't important, a mere frill on his plan.

The plan is, you see, that on handing over as duty master after the film he will walk down the drive to the pub in Paddery Combe. He will see Wither's car still parked on the grass. He will claim at this point to have made his way up to the Temple and found the body, though he will not in fact do so. Thus one set of footprints will be accounted for, coming and going. His explanation for having gone up there will depend on whether he admits to knowing about the elopement, but mere curiosity would be enough. Having waited for a while on the drive he will hurry back to the school and raise the alarm.

So he spends the afternoon doing the chores of duty master. At some point he finds time to abstract my 'gun' and to go out to the garages and smash off an antler tine. The tide continues to flow for him. All the school, bar those helping the hunters, are kept in. Outside staff have their Sundays off. He is most unlikely to be noticed doing these things, and if he is, why, he can always give his plan up. He is committed to nothing, yet.

But the time comes at last. The boys clatter in to the film. Paddery falls silent. Now he goes and makes his weapon, sitting, I think, by an open window facing east so that he can listen for the raucous chatter of the MG's exhaust. He has about an hour, but he needs to leave the thing as late as possible so that it can be almost dark when he reaches the Temple. So, though he hears the car, he waits still. It is dusk when he goes down the drive. He makes no effort to conceal the sound of his footsteps as he trudges up the gravel path. Deliberately he leaves a footprint in one of the soft patches. Wither is at the Temple, looking south, waiting for Annette.

He hears Smith coming, but it is too dark to see that far, so he waits. Smith climbs to the stone platform at the foot of the steps. He stops, calls Wither's name, his voice hushed with conspiracy. A query floats back. Smith gestures to Wither to come down off the skyline. Wither glances south, no sign of Annette's torch on the lake path, descends to hear the presumed message. Smith is carrying a sort of pole.

'What have you got there?'

'Nothing. Found it on my way out. One of the brats has made himself a spear. Too dangerous to leave lying around. Look.'

Automatically Wither cranes in the dusk to inspect the proffered point.

Thrust.

Sorry, I seem to have let the thriller-writer take over. I suppose it's the way I think. Take it that Smith (still allowing that all this is hypothesis) goes back down the path, hurrying so as to give his footprints the impression of just that, then back up to the school to wait for the film show to end. He has his weapon to dispose of. Perhaps he planned to return my 'gun' to its place, but there is now so much blood on it that he realises I will notice. You know, trite though the notion is, I think he simply tossed it and the antler-tine—untied of course—in among the bloody bodies in the garage. Neither would look out of place there, as the gun had been used for deer-carrying, and the blood would be accounted for, superficially. Then, taking his time over it, he walks round outside the building, checking the black-out. There is a chink on the first floor, facing east. When he gets in he goes up and closes it. There is about five minutes left of the film show.

He is coming down the stairs, thinking perhaps that the gamble seems to be coming off, when he is met by a white-faced boy, the one from the conservatory teas, who blurts out about having been to the Temple and found the body. The boy's footprints will be on the path, superimposed on his own. His plan is ruined, his gamble spoilt, his own life now in danger. For a moment the instinct to violence almost breaks out, but then he sees it would be no use. There is a chance yet. He can go down the drive and claim to have climbed the path, as planned. He can meet the headmaster and confirm what the boy has said, then insist that he alone must go and guard the body till the police come, so as to leave the minimum of confusing tracks. On this supposedly second journey up the path, using the torch he has taken from the boy, he can actually look and see whether any of the boy's footprints are in fact on top of his own, and if they are he can attempt to alter the effect by standing accurately into his own print. (All right, it wouldn't stand up to careful forensic inspection, but might with a country sergeant, in wartime, with a death which everybody already assumes is an accident. It doesn't matter, because when he got there he would have found that the question didn't arise, as the boy appeared to have run down from the Temple not on the path but on the grass beside it.)

That's all, except that I never found my gun again.

Isn't writing an extraordinary business? I started this letter almost gaga with horror, despite the whole business being so very much over-and-done-with. Now—at least for the moment—I feel quite calm. It's as though I'd somehow managed to turn what I think are actual events into fiction. When I started I told you I didn't believe any of this rationally, but I did emotionally. Now it's the other way round. Even in the process of writing (as often happens with me) I thought of more and more details which happened to fit in. I think I've actually made quite a fair case. I shall be very interested to know what you make of it, and whether you have any suggestions about how I might check further (other reports of the inquest, find out what happened to Daisy, ditto date of the Smiths' marriage, etc).

But at the same time I now find that at an emotional level the story has become not unreal but non-real. What, five hours ago, was an accumulation of slimy filth inside me has oozed out into sentences and paragraphs, leaving almost nothing behind. Even supposing you were to find in Molly's trunks her account of that evening and thus pretty well prove my theory, I don't think it would make any difference. I would have no instinct to bring Smith to justice, for instance. His act seems to have become somehow aesthetic. If you told me he had saved his soul by it, I wouldn't think you mad. Do you know Auden, *Horae Canonicae*? 'For without a cement of blood (it must be human, it must be innocent) no secular wall will safely stand.' Pernicious nonsense, really.

But do, after all, treat this letter as another instalment of 'light hospital reading', or I shall be sorry to have burdened you with it.

Yours ever,
Paul Rogers

I got to bed nearer five than four and suppose must have slept, but rose feeling as though I hadn't. Yesterday's brightness was gone. I looked out on a garden sodden by a dour thin rain. My own mood had changed too during my brief oblivion. When I re-read my letter to Dobbs over breakfast I thought that the story it told made a sort of sense in a thoroughly contrived way, but that the contrivance was more likely to be mine than Smith's. It all felt extremely literary, even to my current reaction—it was as though in the last twenty-four hours I had been living my normal life in a speeded-up version, had had the idea for a book last afternoon, written it last night, and was now experiencing the familiar post-creative dumps. I didn't change anything, but in the last-but-one paragraph underlined the words, 'His act seems to have become somehow aesthetic' and scrawled 'Rubbish!' in the margin. It is the type of sentiment of which I passionately disapprove. Art is not life.

The post-box is cleared at 9.15, so after breakfast I walked up the lane in a north-east drizzle, posted my first letter and picked up my *Guardian* in the village shop. I stayed there to be out of the wet while I waited for the van to come and go, still uncertain whether I was going to post the second letter. From habit I glanced at the headlines, then turned to McAllister's pocket cartoon at the bottom of page one. I was half-way through one of his interminable captions when my eye was caught by a name in the News in Brief column next door. 'Author dies,' it said. 'Simon Dobbs, biographer of Wilde, Conrad and other major writers, died yesterday after a severe illness at the age of 55. Obituary page 2.'

14

It will not have escaped the reader's attention that 'Steen' and 'Dobbs' are not merely invented names, but the names of characters who are only loosely modelled on real people. No two such monuments adorn our literary landscape. And 'Molly Benison' too. There are echoes in her of more than one (I hope) of the rackety beauties of her period, but which of them *is* she? If any?

Is the reader to assume that the whole of this book, with the exception of some decorative details from my childhood, is pure invention, and that the palaver about my 'novel' is only a bit of fashionable fooling around with notions of truth and fiction, fun for some, tedious for most?

Not really. It is all as true as I have been able to make it. I said this on page one, but the phrase is of course ambiguous. Even supposing I had the literary ability to get the whole truth down, there would still have been areas in which I was not able (in another sense) to tell the truth.

As I have explained, it all began when I was writing a quite different book. I was then asked to recall some trivial details about my childhood and found myself almost unable to do so because of a mysterious blanking-out of memory. I then seemed to myself to overcome this problem by casting my memories into fictional form, and started to write an autobiographical novel. But in the course of doing this discovered (or thought I discovered) that the events I was trying to remember added up to a pattern of some horror. At least one of the people involved was still alive, so the laws of libel made it impossible for me to publish my ideas, while the discovery itself made it impossible to finish the novel. And the death of 'Dobbs' seemed to me to close, both practically and emotionally, the possibility of further investigat   He had been my reader, the sole audience of my bizarre parade. With him gone there was no point in going on with it.

But it was not quite laid to rest. Writing of any other kind was clearly impossible until all this material had been put into some kind of self-explanatory shape and tidied away. The quickest solution was to botch together a book out of my MS, letters from and to 'Dobbs', and some linking passages. There was clearly no possibility of publication, so I put it all in a drawer and went back to the novel I had abandoned in mid-stream when 'Dobbs' first asked me to remember what I could about 'Molly Benison'. (These quotation marks are a nuisance—perhaps the reader will be good enough to supply them notionally for these last few pages.)

Early on in the book you have in your hands I mention, half-jokingly, my apprehension that 'my encounter with this enticing but ultimately frigid material might have ... the effect of rendering me impotent.' (I have only now noticed the coincidence between this notion and the affair between Molly and Steen.) The apprehension was justified. I got nowhere. The miseries of not being able for weeks on end to produce one bearable page of manuscript are considerable, but too boring to describe. In desperation I got my botched-up documents out of their drawer and sent them to my long-suffering publisher with a note saying that I knew they were no use but she might like to see what I'd been up to. (I suppose I imagined that having one person read the stuff and thus getting it minimally published might somehow appease the obsession which I felt was still blocking my ordinary work.)

I think she can't have read the covering letter, or else thought that my disclaimers were mere self-deprecation. At any rate she seems to have read the book as fiction. Not surprisingly she said she found it 'confusing'—this was still at the stage when everyone had two names, remember—and doubted the wisdom of using real people in quite the way I had; though most of them were dead, there was still the question of taste, and if anyone was alive there might be libel.

But she didn't see why these difficulties shouldn't be cleared up. She made practical proposals, and in general wrote as though she were dealing with a novel which was in its last stages of being tinkered with before acceptance for publication.

I felt extremely reluctant. The question of truth haunted me. I will not say that the ghost of Dobbs stood at my shoulder, but the metaphor will do. I believed that I had come as close as is possible to the truth of a set of past events, and now I was being asked to infect that truth with lies.

My income tax demand came in. The rates had gone up. The clutch of my car burnt out. A gale caused a chimney-stack to fall through my roof, disclosing old timber-rots which the insurance did not cover. I settled down and started to tamper with the truth. I wrote this book.

So how much truth does it contain? Quite a lot, really. Certainly much more than I would ever have expected. But a price has had to be paid, in that I cannot afford to indicate to anyone which bits are true and which are not. If I were to go through someone's copy and underline all the true passages, he would then be able to deduce from these, and from the nature of the passages where I have had to depart from the truth, much of what actually happened; and in that case the whole point of altering anything would be lost. So the price of my publishing as much truth as is possible is that I have to do so in a form where it all has to be read as fiction.

Though it worked out in the end, the process of alteration was extraordinarily hard going. I often felt the whole web coming apart in my hands. Yes, early in the 'novel' there is an account of a girl called Cora making a string-pattern which she named 'Starfish' and which then at the loosing of a single loop unravelled into nothing. Truth is such a web, all its nodes interdependent. Let one fact slip and the rest will go. But I managed to catch enough of them to make my own pattern—if not the original 'Starfish' then at least 'Eskimos Running Away'.

The difficulty was not merely technical. There were days,

weeks, when I nearly gave up. But, still speaking in metaphors, I had unseen help. The monitory presence of Dobbs at my elbow changed; he would at least have understood about the income tax, but that is not what I mean. Other presences joined him, Steen and Daisy O'Connell and writers and artists whose names I do not know, who had had life sucked out of their work, books never finished or stillborn, years of creative work aborted or not begun, because of Molly Benison. Was she to do this to me also, even to my tiny volume? She must, somewhere, be defeated.

All very fanciful. Romantic twaddle. Death to decent writing, maybe. But it got me through, and you have this book in your hands despite her.

See next page for coupon.

Look for the Pantheon International Crime series at your local bookstore or use this coupon to order. [**ALL TITLES IN THE SERIES ARE $2.95.**]

Quantity	Catalog #	Price

$1.00 basic charge for postage and handling	$1.00
25¢ charge per additional book	
Please include applicable sales tax	

Total

Prices shown are publisher's suggested retail price. Any reseller is free to charge whatever price he wishes for books listed. Prices are subject to change without notice.

Send orders to: **Pantheon Books**, PIC 28-2, 201 East 50th St., New York, NY 10022.

Please send me the books I have listed above. I am enclosing $_____ which includes a postage and handling charge of $1.00 for the first book and 25¢ for each additional book, plus applicable sales tax. Please send check or money order in U.S. dollars only. No cash or C.O.Ds accepted. Orders delivered in U.S. only. Please allow 4 weeks for delivery. This offer expires 2/28/85.

Name_____

Address_____

City_____ State _____ Zip _____